TAMING

Zach

A TEAM LOCO NOVEL
AMY SPARLING

TAMING

Zach

A TEAM LOCO NOVEL
AMY SPARLING

CHAPTER 1

ZACH

When I was a little kid, my friend Tommy's dad once said, "Second place is the first loser."

We'd laughed and latched onto the phrase, throwing it back and forth at each other every time one of us would beat the other one in a friendly dirt bike race. I know it's stupid to think like that because even getting second place in a race filled with expert riders is still a pretty good accomplishment. People have had extremely well-paying careers from getting second place.

But if second place is the first loser, then what does that make eleventh place?

I reach for a box that I've stuffed too full of my belongings, and not only is it heavy as hell but it's going to explode out the bottom if I don't hold it carefully. With a sigh, I lug the thing out of my apartment and down to my truck, which is also overflowing with the rest of my stuff. How did I get so much stuff? I barely even lived in this place after spending the last two years on the road with my motocross team.

After my devastating screw up two weeks ago, I realized I can't afford to keep this place. It was my pride and joy, too. My first apartment, deep in the heart of Nashville, Tennessee. It was good to me. Many parties were thrown. Many hot girls had a drink in this kitchen. Most of them woke up here the next morning because I'm too damn nice to kick them out after hooking up.

With the last box in my truck, I head back up apartment 312 and do one final sweep of the place to make sure it's empty before I drop the keys off at the front office. I had a professional housecleaner come yesterday and make the place sparkle. I need that thousand dollar deposit back, even though I hate to admit it to myself. I'm broke. Well, nearly broke.

Due to my own stupidity, I am the tenth loser of the summer qualifiers, and now I'm jobless and have no money coming in.

Feeling like the dumbass I am, I get on the highway and leave Nashville in my rear view mirror. I'm heading back home. Back to Hopewell, Tennessee. The smallest country town you'll ever see. If not for Hopewell Motocross Track, no one would even know the place exists. I spent the first nineteen years of my life trying to get out of there, and now just two years later, I'm coming back, broke and jobless and a complete failure.

It's not all over, not yet at least. I'm still a member of Team Loco. I'm still considered a professional motocross racer. I just failed to qualify for the summer circuit, and now I'm stuck sitting on my ass until the fall qualifiers roll around. If I don't make those, then I'll be screwed, and I'll no doubt lose my spot on Team Loco.

I grip the steering wheel as I stare ahead at the highway, telling myself this is just a temporary setback. I still have money, just not enough to justify staying in my apartment for three months while I'm not earning anything. I briefly mentioned the idea of moving back with my mom and she got so damn excited that I knew I had to do it.

Mom's the best woman on the planet. She raised me all by herself after my bastard of a father left her six months pregnant. Her parents both died young, so I've never had any grandparents. I have one aunt, but she lives in Florida and is so antisocial she just keeps to herself. She was also in college when Mom got pregnant with me, so she never helped out. Mom did it all by herself. She was twenty years old with baby me, and she worked her ass off to give me everything I wanted. We never had it too good, and there were many times we ate PB&J every night for dinner, but I'll never be able to pay my mom back for what she did give me.

Motocross.

I was five years old and every time we drove past Hopewell MX park, I'd press myself to the glass and stare in awe at the bikes as they soared over the track.

I wanted to ride. I wanted my own bike. I could feel it in my bones that this is what I was meant to do.

There's no way we could afford it, but somehow Mom bought me a used KTM 50cc dirt bike. She loaded it into the back of her Suburban and we went to the track. She asked a random guy to help us out, and he ended up being Tommy's dad, Big Tom.

Big Tom took me under his wing and taught me how to ride. How to kickstart a bike and shift gears. He kept my bike maintained for me until I was old enough to change my own oil and air filters and tires. When I got too big, he found a great deal on a Yamaha 125 for me and I didn't find out until later that Big Tom bought the thing and my mom made payments to him for years to get it paid off. Big Tom believed in me, probably more than he believed in his own son since Tommy was never very fast. He and my mom were my biggest supporters.

When I was thirteen, I was old enough to work as a flagger at the track, and that helped pay my registration fees for the weekend races. Mom got me used motocross gear at local thrift stores and somehow we made it work. She never had any hobbies of her own, and instead just made sure I was at the track every weekend so I could race. She even traded the Suburban in for an old Chevy truck to haul around my bike.

Thinking about my mom now is the reason I feel so damn shitty. I did all of this for her. Sure, riding is my life and my biggest passion, but I want to be pro for her. I want the big paychecks so I can buy her the new car she deserves so she can finally stop driving around the POS truck of hers. I want to pay off the mortgage on our tiny two bedroom home and then buy her a new house. I want to pay her back for all the years she sacrificed to give me what I wanted. And I was doing pretty damn good for the last two years until it all fell apart.

Marcus, my team manager, has told me a million times that I've got potential. That I've got what it takes. That I could win more if I only stopped the flirting and the partying. I thought he was just being the nagging father figure of the team, but he was right. Dammit, he was right, and I hate admitting it.

I screwed up.

I am the reason I failed.

I let the sudden fame of being the hotshot pro racer on Team Loco get to my head. I stopped working out every day, stopped riding six hours a day to get faster. I slacked on everything except the interviews, the autographing posters for fans, and then using my motocross fame to hook up with the hottest girl at the party.

It was fun as hell, too. But then it came back to bite me.

There are three qualifying races before each season. Even as an official pro rider, you're not guaranteed a spot in the season. You have to qualify by placing in the top 10 in one of the races. You've got three chances.

I blew every single one.

Now my teammates, Jett, Aiden, and Clay will be traveling around the country this summer racing each weekend and earing five to ten grand each time. They'll get the TV interviews and magazine articles and girls throwing themselves at them.

I've got three months of jack shit waiting on me in Hopewell.

But Marcus told me this is a good thing. He told me to get my head back in the game. To hit up the local MX track every damn day and ride like my job depends on it—because it does. I need to work out more, eat healthier, and stay far away from girls. If I get back to top racing condition, then I'll qualify for the fall circuit easily and I'll be back racing with my team. I'll earn the money and get noticed in the big leagues and hopefully drafted to a bigger team. I love Team Loco, but they're the amateur pro team, for racers aged eighteen to twenty-four. Once you're good enough, you get a spot on the real pros. That's where the real money comes in.

I was seven years old when I saw a video of Ricky Carmichael giving a tour of his house. He'd framed the first paycheck he got from his first pro riding team. It was a hundred grand. And that was fifteen years ago. Now the salary is closer to two hundred and fifty thousand. And that's not counting endorsements, sponsorships and paid interviews.

I can take care of my mom with that kind of money. All I have to do is stay focused.

My old house looks just as I remember it as I pull into the gravel driveway. The grass is a little high and I make a mental note to mow it this afternoon so Mom doesn't have to. The two bedroom brick home is about the size of my old apartment, except it has a nice patio on the back that's perfect for entertaining.

I knock on the front door instead of letting myself inside so I don't give Mom a heart attack. She throws open the door and immediately bursts into tears.

"Zach, baby!" she says, throwing her arms around me. "Oh, I missed you so much."

Mom's a whole head shorter than me, and she still smells like flowers. Her brown hair has always been dyed blonde, but now it's kind of a mixture of both colors. Highlights, I guess.

"I missed you too, Mom," I say. I guess I haven't been back to visit her as much as I should.

"I'm so glad you're here," she says, finally letting me go. "Your room is right where you left it."

I smile and glance around the living room. Not much has changed since I was here last Christmas. The same old furniture, and the same framed pictures of me on the wall. There's a few school pictures and my high school graduation one, but it's mostly pictures of me on a dirt bike. A cluster of trophies as tall as my mom are in the corner of the living room. I head down the hall to my room and can't help but snort a bit when I walk in.

I've still got my twin sized bed, but at least I ditched the Power Rangers sheets when I was in high school. All my friends had bigger beds, but stuff like that costs money so I never asked for a new one. It's uncomfortable as hell. I wish I'd thought to keep my bed from my apartment and bring it here instead of selling it with all of my other furniture. Dirt bike posters hang on the wall, and most of my old junk is still in here. It looks like the bedroom of a fifteen-year-old. Part of me wants to update it, but that would mean I'm settling in. If I settle in then I won't go back to racing.

This is just temporary, I tell myself.

After I've unloaded my stuff into my small bedroom, I sit with Mom on the couch. "Are you hungry?"

"I could eat," she says. "I can make us something. What would you like?"

"Nah, don't cook. I'll go get us some food. What about Skeeter's?"

Skeeter's is the best restaurant in town, and besides one name brand fast food joint, it's the only restaurant in town.

"Sounds good," Mom says. "I'll take my usual."

I kiss her on the cheek and then get back in my truck. Skeeter's makes the best cheeseburgers and fries, which is what Mom and I both consider the usual. The restaurant is just how I remember it—old but charming—and I walk up to the bar and order our food to-go.

"Duuude!" a voice I'll always recognize says. I turn and see Tommy sitting a few barstools down. "Zach's back in town!"

"Hey, man," I say, giving him a quick hug. Tommy never pursued professional racing. He always just liked riding for fun. He's gained a beer belly since I last saw him, but otherwise, he's that same goofy kid I grew up with.

"What's been going on?" I ask.

"Same old shit, different day," he says. He points to the embroidered nametag on his shirt. "I've been working out at my uncle's shop for a year now. I think I've finally talked him into letting me buy half the company and be his partner."

"Nice," I say. Tommy's uncle's mechanic shop always gave my mom a good price whenever she needed her car fixed. I've got huge respect for the guy.

Tommy grabs three fries and takes a bite out of them at once. "What's up with you?"

This is the question I've been dreading. The question I will no doubt hear from every person I run into this summer. Why is the famous guy who got out of this small town back in the small town? I'll make up a lie for everyone else, but Tommy is my friend. I swallow my pride and tell him the truth. He listens carefully and doesn't look like he thinks any less of me when I'm finished.

"Ah, man, that ain't nothing to worry about," he says. "You'll get back on the fall circuit."

"I hope so," I say. "I just need to concentrate this summer and find a job or something so I don't drain my savings."

Tommy lifts an eyebrow. "A job? Why waste your time on that when you can just get paid every Friday?"

"What do you mean?" I say.

He snorts. "Man, you've been gone a while. I'm talking about the Hopewell MX summer series. Races every Friday. Sign up for the cash class and you'll win that five hundo every race, easy. You know no one in this state can beat you." He snaps his fingers. "Easy money."

A small flame ignites in my chest. I hadn't thought of that. Although I fully plan on practicing at Hopewell MX all summer to hone my racing skills, I never thought about actually racing. But they do have a summer series here every year. Because it's an amateur track open to the public, there's no qualifying. And if you sign up for the cash class, which is one special race every race day, the winner gets five hundred dollars. Second place gets two fifty and third gets a hundred. It'd be enough money to pay my bills, and I'd be sticking to my goal of getting my life together this summer.

"That's a great idea," I say.

"Hell yeah it is," Tommy says, clapping me on the shoulder. "Just keep your dick in your pants and get back to racing and you'll be back in the pros in no time."

He's right. He's totally right.

I just need to follow through with it.

CHAPTER 2

Bree

I peek outside and look on the front porch. My text alerts said the package was just delivered, but there's only a couple of potted ferns by the door. And I'm not expecting a potted fern.

I look out at the gravel driveway as the sound of dirt bikes echo in the distance. Then I see my package.

It's floating on top of the mailbox. What the hell?

I slip on Mama's flip-flops that she left by the door and make my way down there. The package isn't magical like I first assumed. The mailman must have been too lazy to walk it up to the door so he stuck it on top of our metal mailbox and stretched a big rubber band around it so that it would stay. The rubber band snaps apart as I try to pry it off my mailbox, and the sting of it hitting my wrist makes me curse under my breath. I guess this is my fault for expecting something a little more spectacular. It's not like this package is carrying a Pulitzer Prize or anything.

I rip it open and the padded envelope falls to the ground. I slide my fingers over the fake black leather and lift it up. My heart warms when I see my name— Bree Elizabeth Grayson—printed in an esteemed calligraphy font.

My college diploma.

I tuck it up against my chest, grab the packaging off the ground, and rush back into my house. It's just an associate's degree, and it's just from a community college, but I'm still proud of it. It's the first of its kind in my family.

Both of my parents only have a high school education. They're happy people, and they seem to enjoy our simple life, but it's not the life I want for myself. Mom is smart and probably could have gone to college, but her English isn't the best and that makes her quiet and reserved. She once told me she never even bothered looking into college because she couldn't afford it. But I could see it in her eyes that part of her probably regrets that decision.

My dad never cared for higher education. He got a job here at Hopewell Motocross Park when he was in high school and has kept it ever since. That's why we live here, in a twenty-year-old mobile home set up on the edge of the park grounds. My dad's the groundskeeper. He runs the tractors and the water trucks and he keeps the motocross track in perfect condition. In exchange for a pretty crappy salary, we get to live here for free.

Mom cleans houses fulltime. She takes pride in her job and her clients love her, but I've spent most of my life wishing she didn't have to work so hard. In my senior year of high school I applied for every scholarship I could find. Every time I filled out those forms and wrote those essays, I was picturing my mom coming home from a long day of cleaning up other people's messes, her long black hair all frizzy and unkempt, her hands dried out from cleaning chemicals, and her feet aching.

It worked. I got a full ride to the local community college for a two-year degree, and I just finished my associate's degree in business.

And yet somehow, I still don't have a damn job.

I work at the track on race days and I help Mama clean houses, but that's not a job. I started applying to every salary-paying office position I could find about a month before I graduated. I haven't even gotten an interview anywhere.

All of the good jobs require a bachelor's degree.

All of the not so good jobs also require a bachelor's degree.

I wish someone had told me that this two-year business degree is pretty much worthless. This isn't how my life was supposed to go. I was supposed to get a degree, get a good job, and buy my parents a better house. Buy Mama a better car. Get that knee surgery my dad desperately needs.

But it turns out I'm only halfway there, and the second half of the degree I need is so far away I don't think it'll ever happen.

Bachelor degrees are expensive, and the closest state college is two hours away. Since I can't drive that far every day, I'd have to live in a dorm and I don't even want to think about what that costs.

My parents are heavily against debt of all kinds, even student loans. *Especially* student loans, Mama always says. All of her friends are in their forties and still paying them off. It's not worth it, she always tells me. You know what else isn't worth it? Going into tons of debt and not living at home. My parents need me here. I help out around the house and I work at the track and I make sure Mama doesn't spend more than eight hours a day cleaning houses because I help her get the jobs done quicker. I can't just leave my parents and head off to college.

I walk into the kitchen and throw away the packaging trash and stare at my diploma, wondering if I should just throw it away, too. It's as good as garbage. No one wants to hire the girl with a two-year degree when there are loads of other girls with four-year degrees applying for the same job. I just spent the last two years of my life working toward something that's pretty much worthless if I can't afford the next two years of college.

I swallow the lump in my throat. I'd been so excited to get this stupid thing in the mail and now I wish I'd never even bothered.

The front door closes and I turn around, but it's too late. Mama's eyes light up and she rushes toward me, bringing a cloud of bleach smell with her.

"Is that what I think it is?" she says in heavily accented English. I'm holding the diploma behind my back and I shrug.

She reaches behind me and snatches it from my hands. She marvels at the shiny black case it comes in, probably looking just like I did when I was standing at the mailbox seeing it for the first time. It *is* pretty nice looking. Black and crisp with golden lettering embossed on top. Classy and important.

Mom opens it and her eyes tear up as she reads my name on the diploma.

"I'm so very proud of you, hija," she says softly. "Our first college graduate."

"Community college," I say. "And it's an associate's."

Mom's dark eyes stare into mine. We are exactly the same height. Dad always says I look just like she did when she was a teenager, but I don't believe him. I've seen pictures of her and she was much more beautiful.

"It is still a great achievement," Mama says. "We're going to celebrate!"

While we wait for Dad to get home from work, I hang out in my room and look for jobs on my laptop. I've got all of the major job posting sites bookmarked and I visit them every day. I also have email alerts turned on for new jobs, but I don't trust them. I have to check every day just in case. Maybe one of these days something good will come up, and they'll like my resume, and they'll take a chance on the girl with the two-year degree. I'm still job searching an hour later when Dad gets home and Mama tells him the good news about my diploma arriving. It's kind of funny because I've technically been graduated two weeks now, and that piece of paper is just a formality. But Dad pops his head in my room and he's wearing a big grin. "Proud of you kid."

I roll my eyes. "It's not a big deal."

"It's totally a big deal," he says. My dad is a tall, friendly white guy who managed to win my mama's heart over back when they were sophomores in high school. She was in ESL classes and he desperately needed a Spanish tutor. My dad is always happy and upbeat and sometimes he's kind of goofy and embarrassing, but whatever he did back then really won over my mom and they've been together ever since.

Dad's smile never fades when he's around her. He's giving me the same smile now. "Get dressed. We're going to out dinner to celebrate."

La Tapita is the best Mexican restaurant in the state, and it also happens to be in Hopewell. It opened up about six months ago, and the whole town is crazy about it. They have delicious food that's fresh and handmade and so much better than anything from

Skeeter's diner, which up until now had been the best place to eat.

It's Thursday, which sucks because on Friday nights they have a live mariachi band, but with the way my parents are so freaking excited about my diploma, maybe I can talk them into coming here tomorrow to keep the celebration rolling.

Mama looks beautiful in a dark blue sundress, and her hair falls down her back in soft waves. She looks so much younger when she's not wearing the scrubs she wears to clean houses. Dad has also dressed up for the occasion, wearing a clean pair of Wrangler jeans that don't have any holes or oil stains on them. It might not seem like much, but since he spends his whole day outside working at the track, this is actually dressed up for him.

My parents gush about my degree and how all those long nights I spent working on essays or studying for exams have paid off. I don't want to burst their bubble, so I just smile and nod along, but I wish I could tell them their pride is for nothing. I can't get a job with this stupid degree.

"I've been filling out applications all week," I say when I finally can't take their compliments anymore. "I still don't have any interviews yet."

"Give it time," Mama says.

"I hear the job market sucks for everyone," Dad says. "I was talking with Bryan Appleton the other day—you remember him?" he says to Mama, who nods. "He owns that pool supply store? He said he had one job opening for a cashier and it only pays minimum wage and yet three hundred people applied for it."

"Wow," Mama says. She puts a hand on my arm. "Don't get discouraged, Mi Amor. You'll get a job, even if it takes a while."

I smile back at her, hoping it looks convincing. Mama doesn't know what my true intentions are. That I've made it my life's mission to be successful so that I can take care of them as they get older. As far as my parents are concerned, I can live with them forever if I want and their lives can stay exactly the same.

But I don't want that. I want them to have a real house with a real front yard that's not a dirt bike track. I want them to have a deed with their name on it. And I want the same thing for me, someday.

"You'll never guess who's back," Dad says after the conversation has finally drifted away from me and my accomplishment.

Mom listens intently but I eat a bite of my enchiladas and I'm not really paying attention.

"Zach Pena. Remember him?"

I look up, suddenly very interested. Mom nods slowly. "I think so. Didn't his mom make the blueberry muffins that were so good?"

Dad laughs. "Of course you would remember that part. Yeah, that's him. He was fast as hell and went pro a couple years ago. He was out at the track today. I didn't get a chance to talk to him, but Big Tom told me he's back in town. Everyone's all excited."

"Are you sure?" I ask.

"Yep," Dad says.

Zach Pena was my biggest crush in junior high.

And high school.

And, well, pretty much until the day he signed his Team Loco contract and moved away.

But he never knew I existed, I don't think. We never talked even though I spent my childhood at the track and so did he. I'd be lying if I said I didn't watch his interviews on YouTube every now and then. He's only gotten hotter as he got older. And he's our little town's claim to fame. The first and only racer from Hopewell who made it to the pros.

I stare at my food and try to act casual. "I wonder why he's here?"

Dad shrugs. "No clue. Probably just visiting his mom or something. But Big Tom said someone saw him moving boxes into her house. Maybe he's back for good."

That doesn't make any sense. Zach Pena was one of the lucky ones who found a way to make it out of this small pointless town.

Why on earth would he ever come back?

CHAPTER 3

ZACH

I thought about it all night.

Going from traveling around the country with a race team and racing in the biggest stadiums, at the most popular tracks, to racing at my hometown track in the middle of nowhere? Lame.

It's more than lame. It's pathetic.

But Tommy seemed to think it was a good idea. I'm still just an amateur pro. I know those two words sound like they don't fit together, but there are only about fifty actual professional racers out there. They're all much older than we are on Team Loco and they're legit celebrities. We're amateur pros, which means we're still too young to be official pros, and we're still working toward becoming one of the best. There's probably three hundred of us. We race the 250 class while the real pros race the 450 class. It's a shame too, because I love a 450 dirt bike. They're fast as hell and sound like a dream when you pin the throttle.

So, it's not like me coming home and racing at Hopewell MX Park is the same thing as say, George Clooney going to his hometown and auditioning for the school play. I'm not even really that famous in the motocross scene.

I think about my teammate Jett Adams, and he totally goes home and races at his local track. The locals love him for it. So that strengthens my resolve. I'm going to race the Hopewell summer circuit.

The cash class is the only one of it's kind, and it pays out big. The rest of the races are divided up into several classes (or motos, as they're often called) ranging from bike size to age. As a little kid, I started racing in the 50cc class, and then moved up as my bike got bigger and I got older. They have all kinds of motos, from a women's class to an old people class.

The Over 50 class is what it's called, and that's the most entertaining to watch. It's a bunch of older dudes racing as fast as they can on their vintage bikes.

All of these classes cost a fee to enter, but all you win is a trophy and bragging rights. The cash class, though, is different. There's only one cash class each race day and the winner gets five hundred dollars. People always stay to watch the cash class because only the fastest racers around will sign up to race it. If you're looking for a battle of speed and talent, that's the race to watch.

Five hundred bucks a week isn't bad. It's much less than I'd earn on Team Loco's summer circuit, but it's enough to keep my bills paid and allow me to keep my savings intact.

Plus it's perfectly aligned with my summer goal. I'm already planning on spending every day at the track working on my skills and strength conditioning. This will just be an added bonus, and it'll keep me focused on the win. I can't slack off this summer. I can't lose focus, and I can't do anything to jeopardize my spot on Team Loco.

This whole summer is about one thing: motocross.

Mom has already gone to work when I get out of bed. I check the time, and it's only eight, but she has to leave sooner than that to get to the city for work. She's an accountant for a small business and if you ask me, they don't pay her nearly enough to drive an hour to work each day.

I make some coffee and eat a bowl of oatmeal. I hate this boring shit, but it's carbs and carbs give you a boost of energy before riding. I also scramble some eggs and down them quickly. Twenty minutes later, I'm itching to get on my bike.

The garage door opener has been busted for years. First up on my list of helping Mom is to have it fixed. I lift the metal door manually and it slowly creaks its way up the railing, revealing our small one car garage. All the air whooshes out of my lungs when I see the state of my old bike.

Today is Friday, and I'd planned on racing in tonight's race which is the first of the summer circuit.

But this old thing is filthy. I can't even remember the last time I cranked it up.

Once I joined Team Loco, I got a factory bike that had over twenty thousand dollars in upgrades on it. The best suspension, the leanest cylinders, and the fastest exhaust system they make. Everything on my Team Loco bike is finely tuned to my body. From the handlebars to the suspension, it's all perfectly matched to my six foot one inch height and two hundred pounds. Every millimeter of a professional bike is designed to make the rider go as fast as possible. Only that bike belongs to Team Loco, not me.

My old bike is about as basic as it gets. I remember when I bought this. It's a 2014 Yamaha 250f, and it took me years to save up enough money to buy it brand new from the dealership. Up until then, my entire life had been spent riding used bikes. This one was shiny and new and it was my baby. I won a lot of races on it. I qualified for my spot on Team Loco with this bike.

I look at it now, sitting on the aluminum stand, covered in a fine gritty dirt from being abandoned in the garage for so long. My bright orange handlebar grips have turned yellow and brown from age. The tires are a little flat. Compared to my gorgeous Team Loco bike with custom graphics and detailing, this thing looks like a hunk of garbage.

I run my hand down the leather seat. "Sorry I let this happen to you," I say. It feels stupid talking to an inanimate dirt bike, but my heart aches all the same. This thing is a reminder of where I came from. And what I've lost. And where I want to go back to.

I turn on the dusty old stereo in the corner and crank up some music, then get to work.

The tires are dry-rotted and useless, so I yank them off and toss them in the back of my truck. I clean the carburetor, replace the spark plug, drain the gas and toss the gas can in my truck too. I wipe down the whole bike to clean it, and then I head to the nearby tire shop. It's right next to Hopewell MX Park, and although they service cars and all types of vehicles, they're the unofficial mechanic for the motocross track.

Tommy brightens when he sees me walk in. I'd forgotten he works here now, since all morning I've only been focused on my bike.

"Dude, I'm psyched," he says when he sees the old tires in my hand. "You getting the bike ready to race?"

"I hope so," I say. "The thing hasn't been started in two years."

"We'll get you fixed up," Tommy says. He steps behind the service counter and types quickly on the computer in front of him. "What all do you need?"

"Tires, oil, race fuel if you have any, maybe a new air filter."

"Gotcha," Tommy says.

He rings me up and gives me the friends and family discount. Even though we're both twenty-one years old now, he still acts like the kid I grew up with. He gets way too excited over pointless things. But I guess I could use the motivation right now.

I bring everything back home and finish giving my bike a much needed tune-up. Then I climb up on it and pull out the kick starter and hold my breath. This is it.

I haven't worked on my own bikes in two years. Team Loco has the best mechanics around to do everything for us. All we do is ride. I hope I remembered everything.

I put my foot on the kick starter and give it a swift kick. The engine turns over immediately and roars to life. The sound is deafening in this tiny garage but I grin as I rev the throttle and listen to my baby purr.

"Thank you," I murmur under my breath. I don't know if I'm talking to God or the bike or my own hard work, but I'm happy as hell that my bike is running. Now I just need to hit up the races and win my five hundred bucks.

The smell of exhaust fills the air and it's the greatest smell in the world, besides maybe the smell of a beautiful woman. But women are officially off the agenda this summer, no matter how much that hurts me. It might damn well kill me to keep my eyes on the track instead of on girls, but it's something I have to do.

I park my truck a little further away from the rest of the people here. The races start in three hours, so most of the early arrivals are also racers, here to get a few practice laps in before the races begin. In time, this place will fill up with cars and spectators. I remember it all so well, even though I haven't been to a small town track in forever. I'm used to private entrances and seeing the spectators cheering from stadium seats.

I let down my tailgate and slide out the ramp, then take my bike down. This whole thing is humbling because I haven't done any of this stuff in so long. We used to arrive at the races and all of our stuff was already set out for us by the people Team Loco hires to take care of it all. Hell, sometimes they'd have women dab powder on our faces for photoshoots.

Maybe I was acting like a famous prick—Marcus's words, not mine. Maybe I need this trip back home to remind me of where I came from.

Seeing Mom's shitty furniture at home was enough to remind me of what I'm working towards. It's not all about me. I'm working my ass off to give her a better life, too. One day I'll be an official pro. I'll make the big bucks and Mom can retire early.

I unpack my riding gear and slip into my riding pants, but keep my Adidas shoes on for now. My riding boots are too damn heavy to walk around in. I also leave my shirt off because it's hot as shit out here, even though it's only the start of summer.

Before I can ride, I have to go sign in and register for the races. I make my way toward the white two story building at the front of the park.

"Well look who it is."

I turn and notice Mr. Grayson approaching me, wearing a big ass grin. I don't think he's much older than my mom, but damn he's aged. Probably from spending all day every day out here in the sun. Mr. Grayson works the track grounds, and he's been here as long as I can remember. When I was around eight years old, my handlebars broke when I was at the far end of the track. I was sweating my ass off and exhausted as I pushed the stupid bike back, until Mr. Grayson saw me. He rushed up and helped me roll that bike all the way back to my mom's truck. He's a good guy.

"Hey, Mr. Grayson," I say. "How have you been?"

"Call me Josh," he says, patting me on the back. "You're all grown up now, so no need for this Mister stuff. I heard you were back in town. It's good to see you."

"Yeah, just for the summer," I say.

"I bet your momma's happy to see you."

I nod. "Oh yeah. She's very excited. I should have come back a long time ago."

I feel shitty as I say it—acting like my coming back home for the summer was done out of kindness and not out of failure. Mr. Grayson doesn't seem to notice.

"I'm glad to see you too. We got a couple of boys who have real potential, and maybe all they need is to see you kicking some ass on their home track. You know what I mean? You're the only kid who ever made it out of this town and went pro, and I bet you'll inspire some kids."

"That'd be cool," I say, feeling a little awkward for getting so much praise. I'm a failure—I'm not really in a position to inspire anyone.

"Well good luck son," he says, giving me a weathered smile. "I gotta get back on the tractor before the boss man bitches."

I'm still not at the registration building when I get stopped again. Tommy rolls up in a golf cart, which is a staple at all motocross parks. The sixty acre park is just too far to walk around for most people, so they bring a golf cart or four wheeler to get around.

"Heading to register?" Tommy asks.

I nod and jog to the other side of the cart. He pats the seat next to him. "Hop on in."

"Damn you're fit as hell," Tommy says, admiring my bare chest as he drives the golf cart. "Teach me your ways, man."

I snort. "Hit the gym every day. Eat the right food. Take the right supplements." I lean over and smack him in the gut. "No more beer."

"Aww, hell no," he says with a laugh. "I ain't giving up my beer. I'll just stay fat. Seriously though, it's cool that you're back in town."

"It's not as bad as I thought it would be," I admit. It's only been one day though, but at least I'm back on the track where I belong. Tommy pulls up to the registration building, parking his cart next to two others.

Just when I think this summer will be easy, I notice a girl walking alongside the building. Her long brown hair hangs in a low ponytail that almost reaches the short ass denim shorts she's wearing. Her shirt has Hopewell's logo on it and I'm guessing she works here.

She carries a long roll of those plastic multi-colored triangle flags that make a border around the track. She stops at the corner of the building and bends over, revealing that gorgeous ass as she unrolls some of the banners and ties them to a wooden stake in the ground.

"Dude," Tommy says, startling me out of hot girl hypnosis. He punches me on the arm—hard. "Keep your eyes off the chicks. You're staying focused this summer, remember?"

I nod, but my throat is dry. My riding pants tighten at the image of her bending over like that. She's more than just an ass though, she's gorgeous. She stands up and brushes some stray hairs from her face, then walks toward another stake in the ground.

I look back at Tommy before she bends over again. Seeing his goofy face kills my boner in no time.

I exhale. "You're right. No girls."

But damn, that one was smoking hot.

It's going to take a lot to keep her off my mind.

CHAPTER 4

Bree

Not only do I literally live on the park grounds at Hopewell, but I also consider it my home. Which is why it's so hard for me to follow some of the stupid rules. Grant, the owner of the track, got tired of replacing the plastic flag banners every few years, so he decided that we should put them up and take them down after every race. It's a ridiculous waste of time, and because I'm the youngest and quickest employee they've got, the task always falls on me.

I once looked up the cost of these banners online and it was only a hundred dollars for enough yards to cover the entire track. Once I have the money, I'm going to buy Grant so many rolls of plastic flag banners that he'll never need to worry about them again, and we can keep them up all year. So what if they get a little weathered after a few months? No one comes here for the multi-colored flags. They come here for the racing.

"Bree? Honey, come here!"

I turn around and see Mrs. Sam, Grant's wife, standing inside the doorway of the registration building. Her eyes are closed and yet she's still holding a hand up to shield them from the sun. "Bree?"

"Yes, ma'am," I say, dropping the flags and running toward her. "I'm here."

"Oh thank God," she says, reaching her hands out until one of them lands on my shoulder. She cracks her eyes open just the slightest bit. "I've got a migraine that just came on all of a sudden. It's killing me. Can you take over registration while I go home and lay down?"

"Sure thing," I say, glancing back at my abandoned banners. That's just one more reason why we should leave the damn things up all the time. "Do you want me to take you home?"

"No, no, I'll manage," she says. "I just need my extra dark sunglasses from my car.

She wanders off slowly and I head inside the building. It's a small square building that's maybe the size of a normal house's living room. Not mine, because our mobile home is pretty tiny.

The air conditioning runs at full speed in here, making it a little too cold even when it's hot outside. One half of the room is Mrs. Sam's office, which is just a desk and shelves in the corner of the room. On the other corner is the coffee maker and fridge that's always filled with sodas and vitamin water.

The other half of the building is the registration desk. It has a wall of windows that are counter-height like it's one big drive through window or something. Only instead of driving through, people walk up to it and register for their races on the other side of the window. It's also where racers can pick up their trophies when the races are over.

The window faces the race track, so when you're working up here, you can see a little bit of the races. But the best view is upstairs, where the entire wall is glass. Mrs. Sam's brother is the track announcer and he sits up there every race, watching the finish line and calling out the winners over the track's PA system. He's a pretty funny guy and usually makes jokes all night, but barely anyone pays attention to the speakers overhead.

I climb up on the barstool in front of the registration window, and the fake leather of the seat is freezing cold. It sends chills down my legs. When I was a kid, all the registration was done on paper forms held onto clipboards. But the times have changed, and now it's all done online. Most riders sign themselves up on the website before they get here, but for the people who don't, we hand them an iPad through the window and they sign up themselves. It's pretty easy stuff, and Mrs. Sam always pays me an extra fifty bucks for working registration when she can't.

My friend Meg rushes up to the window. Her normally light brown hair has been dyed hot pink for the summer and she wears it in a messy bun on top of her head. She's wearing a pink tank top that totally clashes with her hair, but that's probably how she intended when she got dressed this morning.

"Bree!" she whisper-yells as she plants both palms on the countertop that separates us. "Oh my God," she says again, glancing behind her real quick. "Did you see who's here?"

I lift an eyebrow. "Who?"

She leans in closer and whispers, "Zach Pena!"

"Oh … yeah, I heard."

I also spent all night watching YouTube videos of his Team Loco races, trying to figure out why he's back here for the summer. But she doesn't need to know that, even if she is my best friend.

"Don't look," she says, keeping her voice low. "But he's right over there."

Of course I look. I don't mean to, but I look, and I see him standing not too far away talking with Little Tom and a few other guys. My heart does this flip in my chest and I don't even know why. There are tons of hot guys at the track every weekend.

Motocross is literally like a breeding ground for sexy, muscular guys.

So why does my chest constrict when it sees Zach Pena?

I know for a fact that he's no good. He's a gigantic player who can be found all over Instagram posing with girls who are much more beautiful than me. And probably much more willing to sleep with him because they're experienced and gorgeous and not some awkward small town girl.

I take a deep breath and try to ignore the butterflies turning in my stomach. "Did you register online?" I ask Meg.

"Just my dad and Logan. But Chase wasn't sure he'd want to race or not, and he decided last minute that he does so—" she slides twenty five dollars cash across the counter to me. "Register that idiot for me, please?"

I laugh. Chase is Meg's little brother, but only by birth order because there's not much little about him.

He's ten months younger than she is and about two feet taller. He's made it his life's mission to annoy her every chance he gets, and I'm telling you, the boy should win an award for how well he's doing it.

I pull him up on the computer and register him for the race, then put the cash in the cash drawer under the counter.

When I look back up at Meg, her eyes are wide and she's frozen solid as if she'd just seen a ghost. "Oh my God!" she whispers again.

Standing right behind her, close enough to touch, is Zach Pena.

She wiggles her eyebrows at me and then waves goodbye. As she turns to walk away, I am suddenly hit with a horrific memory of my childhood. Meg and I were about ten years old and I'd told her about my crush on Zach. We took a notebook from my mom's drawer of business documents and we stayed up all night planning my future wedding to him.

I'd totally forgotten about that entire thing until just now, when Meg gave me that flirty look.

Something tells me she didn't forget it at all.

Little Tom and the guys are still talking a ways away. I kind of wish they would have accompanied Zach to the registration window because then it wouldn't be like staring into the sun to look at him.

And he's shirtless. Holy shit.

Those muscles weren't just airbrushed on for the Team Loco promotional photos online. His blue and gray riding pants hang low on his hips, revealing just a little too much of his ridiculously sexy body.

This kind of hotness should be illegal, because it's making it very hard for me to function.

Still, I put on a polite smile like I do for all the customers. At least, I think that's what my face looks like right now. I've kind of lost all feeling in it.

"Good afternoon," Zach says. His voice is like the smell of coffee when you wake up in the morning. Absolutely perfect. He taps his fingers on the counter in front of him and shakes the dark hair from his eyes. That single head movement makes my entire body blaze on fire. I was freezing cold a few minutes ago, and now I am hot lava. He smiles. "I need to register for the cash class."

I hand over the iPad, my body on autopilot. I take in a ragged breath and tell myself to get it together, *dammit.* I am a woman and I am strong and amazing and I refuse to be the type of pathetic girl who turns to goo when she's talking to a hot guy.

I refuse.

I straighten my back and press my lips together into a flat smile.

"Fill this out," I say. I get a burst of pride when my voice sounds normal and not like a stupid fangirl. "The cash class is thirty dollars. We take cash or credit cards.

"Cool," he says. He opens his wallet and hands me a credit card.

My hand shakes as I swipe it through the card reader, but luckily he's not watching me when I put it back on the counter for him.

He's quiet for a few minutes while he types his information into the iPad. My heart slows down a bit and I allow myself the pleasure of checking out just how gorgeous he his.

His whole chest is like a freaking statue of muscle. I want to reach out and touch it. His dark hair is a little long on top, but it works really well on him. It's shaggy but also somehow neat and tidy. My eyes roam over his hands, his sexy fingers and the veins in his forearms as he works the iPad, but holy hell—I have to look away. The man has perfect hands to go with his perfect chest and perfect face.

Everything about him is perfection, and that gets dangerous. I almost don't blame him for being a womanizer. It's not really his fault that he's so hot that women just fling themselves on him.

That thought brings me back to reality. Zach Pena is not someone I'm allowed to crush on. He's a man whore, in every sense of the word.

He looks up and grins. "They've got you doing flags *and* registration?"

I have no idea how he knows that but I nod.

He hands me the iPad. "You want me to have a word with old man Grant? He's so damn cheap and he should just hire more people."

I shake my head. "Mrs. Sam got sick so I had to take over for her."

"Ah," he says.

Don't look at his lips, don't look at his lips.

He picks up his credit card and slides it back in his wallet. "What's your name?"

"Bree."

"Bree," he says as his blue eyes meet mine. They are the color of the ocean, and just like the ocean, they're swimming with secrets I wish I could know.

He holds my gaze long enough to make me short of breath. "I'm Zach," he finally says.

"Yeah, I know."

Dammit. Why the hell did I say that? Now he knows I'm one of his many admirers.

A small smile tugs at his lips and I shrug, trying to knock that smug look right off his face. "I mean, I thought you might be. People have been talking about your sudden arrival."

He runs a hand through his hair and all I can see are the way his muscles flex in his bicep. "I wish they wouldn't make such a big deal about it. Can't a guy come back to his home track for the summer?"

I shrug again because his hand is still resting on the back of his head, his bicep is still flexed, and apparently I am nothing but a cavewoman whose only instinct is to get me a piece of his gorgeous man.

He lowers his hand. "So what are you doing after this?"

"Going to bed." I feel like an idiot right after I say it, but it's the truth. "These summer races last until after midnight," I add, as if that somehow makes me less of a dork.

He nods, his lips pressing together in a flat smile. I see his eyes roam down my face and then he takes a step back, as if he's suddenly decided something.

Of course he did. I am just some pathetic loser. It shouldn't have taken him that long to figure it out.

"See you around, Bree."

And then he's gone.

And every muscle in my body is on fire.

And my face feels the hottest of all.

CHAPTER 5

ZACH

Damn, that was a cold rejection. I don't think I've ever been rejected at all, much less that quickly. Bree would rather go to bed after the races than hang out with me?

Still, I think I'm grateful that the gorgeous brunette turned me down. As soon as I'd asked what she was doing tonight, I immediately felt that tug of shame in my gut. I'm not supposed to be asking out hot girls. Especially not on my first day back at the races. Maybe Fate is looking out for me because she turned me down and now I can get back to focusing on my goals this summer.

Easier said than done. I can't get Bree's smile out of my mind as I walk back to my truck and get some practice laps in. Within a couple hours, a ton of people arrive, and by the way everyone's coming up to talk to me, I almost wonder if they only came to the races because they heard I'm back.

I shake a ton of hands and catch up with all the people I used to know back when I lived here before I went pro. Some of my old riding buddies are even married with kids now, which is weird as hell. I guess in a small town, there's nothing else to do but settle down once you turn twenty years old. Part of me wonders what that would be like – living the small town life with a woman you love.

I can't even fathom love right now. My whole life has been hookups and one night stands. It's fun, don't get me wrong, but sometimes I wonder what it would be like to wake up to the same girl every morning, knowing you'll never have to be single again.

Bree's face flashes in my mind again and I quickly think of something else. *Anything* else. I stare at the small bikes that are racing on the track and try to focus on that. The cash class is the last race of the evening, so I've got a lot of time to kill.

I'm not going to lie—it does feel good to have all this attention. I walk over to the bleachers to hang out and watch the races and people just swarm all around me.

When I'm with Team Loco, we hang out as a team and we always have people around us, adoring fans as Clay calls them, but they're excited about everyone. Right now it's just me. I'm the center of attention, and the biggest thing to happen to this small town in a long time.

I sit next to Tommy and some guys I grew up with while we watch the races and shoot the shit for a while. I get my fair share of flirty looks from girls as they walk by, and a few ask me to autograph something for them. But the attention doesn't get me as hyped up as it usually does. I can't stop thinking about her.

None of these other girls compare. And some of them are hot, don't get me wrong. Just not that type of hot that Bree is. She's soft and sweet and when she smiles there's a lot of hidden emotions behind her eyes that I'm dying to find out. I don't just want to hook up with this girl, I want her to tell me all those secrets. I like that she works at the track and isn't just some track hoe who hangs out to flirt with guys. She must really enjoy the sport.

I glance toward the registration building wondering if she's still inside. Tommy taps my shoulder and says something and I nod along even though I'm not hearing a word he says.

I can't get her out of my mind.

That sweet smile, those gorgeous lips.

That perfect ass.

Hours later, I'm still thinking about her as I get ready for my race. She's in my mind when I pull on my boots and latch them closed. When I put my shirt on and my helmet and my goggles. When I crank up my bike and ride over to the starting line. My body is on autopilot as I get ready for the race, but my mind is on her.

Maybe I just need to hook up with her. Just once. Just get her out of my system and then I can go on with my life.

The thought turns me on, and then I realize how stupid it would be. What am I supposed to do? Take her back to my twin bed in my mom's house?

Hell no.

As much as I want to hook up with this girl, that is about the *least* sexy way to do it. I miss my apartment. Why, oh why, did I get rid of it?

I line up at the starting line alongside the other twenty guys who are hoping they can beat me in this race and win the money. I lean forward on my bike, revving the engine.

The roar of all the bikes grows in intensity and the vibration of my motor makes my whole body hum. The gate will drop any second and the race will begin.

Still, I'm thinking about her.

Maybe I can hook up with her in the back seat of my truck. It's still pathetic but not as bad as bringing her to my childhood bedroom.

Maybe I just need one night with this girl to get her out of my mind and *then* I can spend my summer focusing on motocross instead of girls.

Yeah, maybe that's all it'll take.

The gate drops and I pin the throttle, easily getting the lead. I'm picturing what it would feel like to make out with her as I round the first turn, and I guess I get too distracted because soon I hear the rumble of an approaching bike. Whoever is in second place is gaining on me, and quickly.

I tell my dick to calm the hell down and I try to focus solely on the race. The track in front of me, the bike that's under my control. This summer racing series is my part time job and I'm going to win it.

One lap down, five to go.

Adrenaline pulses through my body and I pin the throttle, making my old bike soar faster than it's been in years. I keep the lead in the second lap, and then the third. Each lap passes over the finish line jump, which is the biggest jump of the track. It's also right in front of the bleachers where most people hang out to watch the races. I can hear the cheers as I soar over the finish line jump for the fourth lap.

I am famous in my own hometown.

It's not much, but it keeps me pumped. Makes me want to work harder, and get back on Team Loco for the fall. I want to make not just my mom proud, but everyone else in this little country town. I want them to always think of me like this—the racer who was good enough to go pro.

When the checkered flag waves, it feels like no time at all has passed. I throw the bike sideways and do a whip over the finish line, making the crowd cheer as a dozen camera flashes go off.

It feels good to win.

Maybe this summer at home is exactly what I needed. I need to feel the power that comes with winning. The satisfaction that I'm good enough, fast enough, worthy enough to keep pursuing my dream.

Tommy is already waiting at my truck when I get there. I slide off the bike and he takes it from me and puts it on the stand. He's like my hometown pit crew now. I feel bad for not keeping in touch with him more when I was on the road. He's always been a good guy.

I pull off my helmet and set it on my tailgate.

"Whew," I say, flinging the sweat off my hair. Even though it's dark outside, I still get drenched in sweat while racing. It's from a combination of the gear, the exercise, and the adrenaline.

"Lookin' good, man." Tommy grins and hands me a Gatorade from the ice chest in the back of my truck. "Man, I miss the days of seeing you ride. It's so much better in person than watching you on the TV."

"Yeah, because in person I'm in first place," I say with a snort. I crack open the lid of the Gatorade and down it in a few sips.

Half a dozen pre-teen boys rush up to my truck with big ass grins on their faces. I smile and thank them as they dish out compliments. One of them asks me to sign his helmet, and I do, really big right across the back of it. His face lights up when I hand it back.

The next twenty minutes go by like this, my adoring fans all taking turns telling me that I'm a badass. That I inspire them to become pro too someday. I can't lie, it feels pretty damn awesome.

I keep a smile on my face because even though I'd rather go collect my cash and hit the shower, I made a promise to myself when I was sixteen years old, and now I'm sticking to it.

Tommy and I had gone to the professional Supercross races in Nashville. We waited in line for hours to meet our hero, Jack Aldean, who raced for Kawasaki. We even paid for the VIP tickets to get an autograph. By the time we got there he was clearly tired of signing posters and meeting fans and he just acted like a total dick. Like we were ruining his day by being fans. I told myself right then and there that if I ever got famous myself, I'd always value and appreciate my fans. I'd never make them feel like shit for liking me.

So I smile, and shake hands and sign helmets and get down on my knees to talk to the tiny kids who are excited to meet me but too shy to say anything.

I listen to parents tell me how I'm their kid's hero, and I stand and pose for picture after picture until I can barely see anymore over the burn of the camera flashes in my vision.

Eventually the crowds thin out and I make my way to the registration building to collect my winnings. My anticipation wanes when I see the woman behind the glass. It's Mrs. Sam, the owner's wife. I'd been hoping to see someone else.

"Good race," Mrs. Sam says. She slides an envelope over to me and I know it's filled with cash. "Everyone loved seeing you out there. I think we sold twice as many entry tickets just for your adoring fans."

I smile at her even though I'm only thinking of Bree and how disappointed I am that she's not here. It is after midnight though, so maybe she's home sleeping like she said. Although I doubt it. She probably just didn't want anything to do with me.

"Don't forget this," Mrs. Sam says as I start to walk off. She holds up a giant red sparkling trophy. The first place trophies are about three feet tall. She turns it sideways and hands it to me through the window.

When I was a kid, these trophies were better than Christmas morning. I collected each one I got, ranging from eighth place to first place, and I kept them all in my room. Then they overflowed into the hallway and the living room and my mom's room. I always gave her my first place trophies because I wanted her to have the best ones.

Then, somewhere around high school, I stopped caring about them as much. I had bigger goals and dreams and plastic trophies weren't it. I was dreaming about sponsorships and professional paychecks.

I thank her and tell her goodnight, and then I turn to walk back to my truck. Most of the spectators and racers have headed home now, but there are still some people around.

I notice a little boy, probably around five years old. He's standing next to his mom and he's watching me with that same awestruck look I used to give to the older motocross guys.

"Hey, bud," I say, walking over to him. I hold out the trophy and his eyes widen. "This is for you."

"Oh my God," his mom says, putting a hand to her chest. "Are you sure?"

"Yep," I say, handing it over. The boy grins so big it makes me smile. "Have a good night."

Back at my truck, one person is waiting for me. I can tell by the slim body that it's not Tommy, and the bright shock of blonde hair also means it's not Bree.

She leans against my truck, watching me approach. She's probably my age, maybe a little older, and she's wearing a ton of makeup and barely any clothes.

"Zach Pena," she says. "I can't believe we haven't met yet."

"Nice to meet you," I say. I shove the envelope of cash into my glove box and then walk to the back of my truck and lift up the tailgate. My bike is already loaded up, no doubt thanks to Tommy.

"I'm about to head out," I say even though my brain is currently asking WTF is wrong with me. I know why she's here. It's a surefire hookup.

I never turn these down.

She pokes out her bottom lip and walks over to me, putting her hands on my chest. Her nails are long, pink, and fake. "You should take me with you," she says, in full on seductress mode. I wonder where girls get that low sultry voice. They all sound the same.

My heart beats a little quicker, and I know how easy it would be to give in. This is the type of girl I could hook up with in the back of my truck. And she'd be happy about it too.

I even get this sick idea that I could close my eyes and pretend she's Bree, and maybe that'll help me get over her. But I can't do that shit. Not now. Not anymore.

My future depends on me keeping my head in the game. And the game is motocross, not easy women.

I take her hands and carefully lower them from my chest. "Sorry," I say, and part of me actually *is* sorry. And then I use an excuse that someone else already used on me. "I need to get home and go to sleep."

CHAPTER 6

Bree

I try not to yawn, but I don't do a very good job. I wish I had my coffee mug, but I left it in the car because we can't bring it into people's homes. Mama says it's unprofessional. She does everything very professional in her housekeeping business. I'm just glad we only have to wear tan scrubs with Mama's company logo embroidered on it, instead of some stupid uniform. She's so serious with her business that I sometimes fear she'll make me start wearing a maid dress like you see in the movies.

It's Sunday morning, not even noon yet, and Mama and I just arrived at our third house for the day. There are five houses on the schedule and since they're weekly clients, it shouldn't take too long to clean each house.

While Mama works on the kitchen, I take the vacuum around the house and get every carpet cleaned, making sure to leave perfect carpet lines. It's kind of my signature cleaning move—if there is such a thing. I leave all the houses with perfect carpet. The trick is to walk backward as you vacuum so that you don't leave any footprints.

I'm finished in the den and it looks magnificent. This client's antique furniture has been dusted and polished and the drapes have been cleaned and the floor is now pristine.

I stand here for a minute and admire my work, and then some punk kid comes running through the room wearing only swim shorts.

"Bahahaha!" he says, pointing at his footprints on the carpet. "I messed it up!"

I want to smack him on the head with my vacuum, but I smile instead. "Yes, you did."

"Ha-ha," he says again, pointing a finger at me. "Now you have to fix it."

I grit my teeth and unwind the vacuum cord so I can plug it back in and get to work. The kid laughs and runs back out of the room. I hope Mama is done soon so we can get the hell out of here before he purposely messes anything else up.

This is the part of the job I don't like so much. It's annoying when kids treat us like shit, but it's the adults that make it worse. I can't count how many husbands I've seen watch me work from the corner of their eye, giving me this look like I'm *less than*. Like I'm just the hired help who isn't even a real person.

And the women aren't much nicer, either. I swear some of them hire us just so they can boss us around and feel like they have some kind of power in their lives.

But about half of our clients are nice people, and they always make the job feel worth it. I know people look down on maids, but really, my mama has made more money in a year than my dad has several times. And most of her clients pay in cash so she doesn't have to wait for weekly paychecks. It's a steady job with the satisfaction of being self-employed. I just wish everyone respected us.

When the house is clean, I join Mama in her car and I reach for my coffee.

"Ew," she says, curling her nose as she drives. "That stuff is old."

"But it's still delicious," I say, taking a long sip. This stainless steel thermos keeps the coffee hot all day, despite how it was brewed at five a.m. this morning.

"We have a new client today," Mama says, turning onto a road that deviates from our usual Sunday route.

"Oh yeah?" I try not to groan. New clients usually mean a disgusting house that hasn't been cleaned in ages.

Mama must read my mind because she says, "Don't worry, I don't think this woman lives in a pigsty. She lives alone and she's in her forties and said she has arthritis that makes it hard to keep her house clean."

I nod. Living alone means there are no bratty kids to ruin my day. "How did she find out about us?"

Mama shrugs. "Through the grapevine, I guess."

"Mama, we really need to make a business plan. Get a website, social media—the works."

She rolls her eyes just like she does every time I mention this kind of thing. Mama has always run her business through word of mouth and small-town charm. She could take it bigger, though.

"We could be legit," I say, not wanting to give up this easily. "We could grow and get an office in town and hire other housekeepers, and then one day you can work at the office and won't even have to clean anymore."

"That sounds like way too much effort," Mama says, keeping her eyes on the road.

"No, it sounds like a great way to grow your business. Let me help, Mama. I can put my associate's degree to work."

She flattens her lips and looks over at me. "Is that why you keep talking nonsense about making the business bigger?"

"Well, yeah," I say. "I have a degree in business and I could use it to help you. We could become a huge housekeeping company and even expand into other counties. It could be like, a chain."

I'm talking quickly, getting all excited about the possibilities of making Mama's small one-woman operation into a real legit business.

But my mother doesn't see things the way I do. "No," she says, shaking her head. "You need to use your degree for something special. You need to get out there and do something great with your life."

"What could be greater than making a business with you?" I ask. "We're family. We should stick together."

Mama parks on the side of the road in front of a small older home. "We will always stick together, *Mamacita*. But you deserve much bigger things in life. I appreciate your offer, but you need to dream bigger."

She gives me a soft smile and then gets out of her car, ending the conversation for now.

I don't know how she can tell me to dream bigger when I'm stuck in this small town. There isn't anything any bigger to dream about.

With a huff of resignation, I step out of the car and head to the trunk to get all of our cleaning supplies. Mama walks to the front door and a woman lets us inside. She's pale and a little plump with shoulder length hair that's brown with highlights.

"Nice to meet you," the woman says to both of us. "I'll just be in the backyard gardening. Come get me if you need anything."

Awesome. I love it when the homeowner isn't here while we clean. It just makes it awkward to be tidying up someone's home while they're sitting there watching you. The homeowner slips out the back door and Mama and I take stock of the house.

There's a small living room, a smaller kitchen, and a hallway off to the side which probably has the two bedrooms. This place is small and doesn't look very dirty so hopefully it won't take long.

Mama leans closer and talks quietly, even though the lady is outside and can't hear us. "She's a nice woman and this would be an easy client," Mama says. "Let's do a really good job to make sure she asks us to come back next week."

"I always do a good job," I say with a smile. I can tell this means a lot to my mom.

"I'll take the kitchen," she says. Kitchens are her specialty. She can clean an oven like no one's business.

"I'll do the bedrooms and the hall," I say, taking my basket of cleaning supplies with me.

There are some Hopewell Motocross trophies scattered around the house, and that's pretty common here in town. A lot of people ride dirt bikes here. The trophies are a pain in the ass to dust because the little plastic dirt bikes snag on my duster. I'll save them for last.

In the hallway, there are three doors, and two are closed. I hate opening a closed door in a stranger's house, so I venture down to the open doorway and hope that Mama will undertake the door opening before I have to.

One time when I was about thirteen years old, I opened the door to a room that was filled with porcelain dolls. They all had pretty hair and fluffy dresses, so it wasn't like some horror movie scene, but it still scared the shit out of me. You never know what you're gonna find in someone else's house.

The open room at the end of the hall belongs to a little boy. My chest tightens a little bit, because Mama had said this woman lives alone. I wonder if she has custody issues with her son and an ex-husband or something. Or maybe if her son...

Well, I don't want to think about that. The bed looks lived in, and there are clothes on the floor, so I don't think her son passed away. Maybe it's like a nephew who only visits her sometime.

Regardless, the room is a mess. I pick up all the dirty clothes and toss them in a hamper basket that's in the corner of the room. There's dirt bike posters on the walls and a few trophies scattered around. The dresser is covered in dust and it makes me sneeze as I dust it off and then spray some wood cleaner on top. I have to get the vacuum in here to clean the wooden blinds over the windows because they're equally dusty.

Once things are dusted and shining, I head over to the small bed. Sometimes we wash bed sheets for clients, but Mama hadn't said anything about that, so I'll just make this bed and leave the sheets as they are.

I take the top sheet and fluff it up, and the smell of some kind of cologne floats up in the air. It smells good. Not like a little boy, but more like a man. I wonder how old this kid is. I bet all the girls like him because he smells good.

I tuck in the sheets at the corners, making them extra crisp, and then I pull the comforter over and tuck it neatly in all around the edges. I'm a pretty excellent bed maker. If Mama's skill is kitchen ovens, mine is bed making.

When the bed is perfect, I stand back up and glance around the room, seeing if there's anything I might have missed. That's when I notice the man standing in the doorway.

Not a boy.

A man.

I freeze, my mouth open. It's not just any man.

It's Zach Pena, in the flesh. In *lots* of flesh. He's standing there with a black towel wrapped around his waist, hung low enough to show off more than I need to see. His bare chest looks just as good as it did at the track the other day, and his hair is wet and hanging in his eyes.

"Um, hello," he says.

I'm still here, still frozen. I do manage to close my mouth though.

Zach smiles. "Why are you cleaning my room?"

Then his gaze drifts to my chest, and I feel the slightest bit self-conscious but then I realize he's reading the logo embroidered on my scrubs. "Housekeeping?" He looks just as confused as I am.

"The woman who lives here—your mom?" I stutter out, "She hired us. To clean. Today."

God, I feel like an idiot but at least I got out a halfway understandable sentence.

"Oh okay," Zach says. "Sorry, I didn't know."

His lips stretch into an easy grin. "If she'd told me then I wouldn't have walked in here like this. I was in the shower," he says, cocking his head toward the hallway.

"I'm so sorry," I say, finally snapping back into housekeeper mode. This isn't the first time a client has walked in on me having just got out of the shower, and it probably won't be the last. It is, however, the first time someone this gorgeous has stood before me wearing only a towel and that tight line of muscles that points in a V straight to where I shouldn't be looking.

"I'm actually done in here, so I'll get out of your way."

I grab my cleaning supplies and rush toward the door, which he's still blocking. At the last second, he steps to the side to let me through.

"Wait," he says. "Bree, right?"

I nod and I stand here in the doorway, just inches away from this guy who smells like Old Spice deodorant, and my insides are turning warm and tingly just being this close to him.

His tongue flicks across his bottom lip and the motion only lasts a split second, but it seems to go on forever in my mind. Damn, he's hot. Dangerously hot.

His blue eyes seem to sparkle as he says, "You should stay. We can hang out. Talk about motocross."

My heart thunders in my chest. Why is this guy asking me to hang out again? Is this some kind of joke? Is he one of those pricks who thinks that just because I'm the help I should do whatever he says?

I mean, yeah, in a perfect world I would love for someone like Zach to like me. But he's so far out of my league that it'll never be a possibility. He's a famous talented dirt bike racer.

I'm a housekeeper with a useless two-year degree.

"No," I say, stepping into the hallway. It feels much colder out here than in his room.

"Why not?" he says, and he actually looks a little hurt.

I shrug, and tell myself to say something besides *you're out of my league.*

"You're naked," is what my brain chooses to say. My cheeks flush, and I sneak one last glance at his gorgeous body.

And then I take my supplies and leave.

CHAPTER 7

ZACH

I close my bedroom door and sit on my neatly made twin size bed, still wearing a towel and feeling like a total ass. Why did I ask her to stay and hang out?

I'm naked.

I smile a little despite myself, because that's kind of funny. I wasn't thinking about how I'm currently wearing only a towel when I asked her to stay. I was thinking about how she's been running through my mind all damn day. Pretty much since the moment I first saw her at the track. She's been there, a constant thought in my mind that keeps building a desperate need for me to get closer to her.

And of course she has no idea. Which is why she left.

Also, she'd been cleaning my childhood bedroom. What the hell is up with that? She did say she had work in the morning but I never in a million years thought the work she spoke of would be picking up my dirty laundry.

I fall back on my bed and feel my entire body go warm with embarrassment. I can't believe she was in here. I can't believe she saw my dumb childhood room. It totally looks like I live here too, and not that I'm staying for the summer. I've already unpacked my clothes and hung them in the closet. The only thing I haven't done is clean out all my old kid stuff or upgrade my bed.

She's probably got me all figured out now. She knows I failed to secure a racing spot on the summer circuit and now I'm back here, a complete failure, living with my mom like some loser.

I just need to show her that it's not true. I need to find her, talk to her, convince her to go on a date with me. I'll blow a ton of money on a date and tell her that

I purposely took the summer off and let her know that I'll be back on top in the fall. Girls love that shit. They all want to be on the arm of the guy who is famous. I'll prove to her that I am still famous. Still rich. Still good enough for her attention.

Even as I think it, I am almost certain she's not the type of girl who cares about that stuff anyway. If she were, she'd have stayed after work on Friday to go home with me. She would have been at my truck instead of that random blonde girl. If she really wanted me the way I want her, she'd have stayed in my room, pushed the door closed and yanked off my towel.

I'm turned on just thinking about it, and I let my mind wander with the daydream of an alternate reality where that really did happen. Then I hear some people talking and I realize she's probably still here, and I shouldn't be fantasizing about her gorgeous body climbing up on top of mine.

I get up and throw on some clothes and then listen by the door. I hear my mom talking to someone who isn't Bree. This woman has a Spanish accent. I don't hear Bree at all, but after a few minutes, my mom says goodbye and I hear the front door close behind them.

I wait a little longer just to make sure they're gone, then I walk into the living room.

"Uh, Mom?" I say. She's sitting on the couch flipping through channels on the TV. "Why was there a girl cleaning my room when I walked in there after a shower?"

"Oh my," Mom says with a laugh. "Please tell me you didn't scare the poor girl."

I fold my arms over my chest. "Since when do you have a cleaning lady?"

"Since today. Sorry, I forgot to tell you. I keep forgetting you're even here." She smiles at me and I can't be annoyed anymore. "My arthritis is only getting worse and I thought I could use some help around the house. I scheduled for Anna to come back every two weeks, so I'll let you know before she's here again."

Anna must be the name of the other woman who was here. I sit on the couch next to her. "Mom, you need to see a better doctor for your arthritis."

She shrugs and waves me off. "I do see a doctor."

"Yeah, but we need to get you to a good one. Some famous well-known doctor who can treat arthritis with the best methods, not the little town doctors here who don't know shit."

"They all went to medical school, didn't they?" she says. She's being stubborn like she always is when I try to pay for her to have something nice.

I decide to drop the subject for now, but I'll research good arthritis doctors later and see if I can get her an appointment with one.

I lean back on the couch and try to act casual while I pry for information. "So that one girl that was cleaning my room also works at the track. She seems young to work two jobs."

"I think she just helps out at both jobs. It's not a full-time gig."

"Oh yeah? Is she in college or something?"

Mom turns to me, giving me a look that immediately makes me feel guilty even though I don't think I am guilty of anything. "Zach, don't you dare hit on the cleaning girl."

I open my mouth like I'm offended. "What? No... I was just making small talk."

Mom's lips press into a line. "Bree is a smart girl. She just graduated from college and everything. You don't need to go make her your flavor of the week."

I swallow. It's one thing to know you're a player, but to have your mom call you on it is another. "I wasn't going to do that," I say, but my voice has lost all of its defensiveness. "I was just curious."

"Why?" Mom says, glancing at the TV as she chooses a show to watch. "You never cared about the Grayson girl when you were a kid."

"Wait, what?" *The Grayson girl?* "You mean like Mr. Grayson from the track?"

Mom laughs. "Yes, son. That's the little Grayson girl all grown up. She used to sit next to me on the bleachers when you'd race and tell me how great you were. It was obvious she had a crush on you back then, and you're not going to go break her heart now." Mom levels a glare at me. "I mean it, son. She's a good girl. Too good for you to use and then dump to the side like you always do. Promise me you'll stay away from her."

Shame floods over me at the realization that this girl has been in my life way longer than I even realized. I can only barely remember Mr. Grayson having a daughter, and I don't think I ever paid attention to her. Of course, back then, I didn't care about girls. All I cared about was winning.

"I promise," I tell her, and I hate that I know this is one promise I better keep.

By Thursday night I've managed to stick to my goal for four whole days. I woke up early each day, worked out for an hour, went to the track and rode my bike for three hours and then came home and worked out for the rest of the day. I probably have zero body fat now that I've been training so hard. I go to bed early, wake up early, train, and eat right.

It feels like I'm back on Team Loco already, even though I'm still stuck here in Hopewell. I watched the first summer race on TV the other day, but seeing my teammates racing without me wasn't very fun. I only watched a little bit of it before I turned the TV off in frustration and went back out in the garage to use my weight bench.

Now, it's only eight at night, and I've worked out all day but I'm wondering if I should work out some more after I make a protein shake. I have to stay busy or I'll think about her.

My phone rings, and I'm glad to see Tommy's name on the incoming call. I haven't seen him all week.

"Sup man?" I say, pressing the phone to my ear.

"I had a rough day," he says. "Customers pissing me off left and right. You wanna hit up the bar?"

"On a Thursday?" I say with a laugh. I've been twenty-one for six months and it only just now occurred to me that I've never been to a real bar. Fancy overpriced bars at luxury hotels don't exactly count.

"Well Friday is race day so you can't do it then," Tommy says.

"Fair enough. Blues?" I guess, because that's the only bar in town.

"Yeah, see you there."

Hanging out with my boys, drinking beer, and playing pool should be enough to get my mind off the girl who doesn't want me. I'm looking forward to it as I make the short drive over there. The place is packed, even for a Thursday night. I guess barflies don't care what day of the week it is.

I can picture my manager in my mind. Marcus would give me a stern look and tell me not to get too drunk because it'll undo all my hard workouts and healthy eating. He's right, of course, but I've gotta get Bree off my mind somehow.

Since she clearly won't let me sleep with her, I've got to find another way to get her out of my system.

The bar is bigger on the inside than it looks outside. There's a shitty country wannabe band playing in one corner, a few pool tables, and a dance floor.

Tommy and his friends from work all show up, and I forget their names instantly but they all know mine.

We get some beers and snag a pool table. I'm not the best at pool, but I can hold my own. The game keeps getting interrupted by people walking up and talking to me. Some just want to say it's cool to see me again, and I'll vaguely recognize their faces. Some want to stay and chat a while, and it's annoying because I just want to play some pool and relax.

The girls are the worst. Before Tommy and I have even finished our first game of pool, I get three girls coming up to me trying to flirt. Maybe they just want free drinks, or something, but I'm not having it. I'm polite, but I tell them I can't talk because I'm in the middle of a game.

After one girl who is blessed with an amazing rack wanders off, Tommy looks at me and shakes his dead.

"Damn, man. You could get any girl in here, and yet you still turned down the hottest one. I'm impressed."

I inhale a deep breath and exhale. "You know how it is. I gotta keep my head on straight. No girls this summer."

Even as I say it, I don't fully agree with myself. That last girl would have done anything I told her to. She'd probably be a pretty good lay, on par with the girls who hang out in the professional motocross circle. Those kinds of girls are just like us guys—they only want one thing. They won't be staying overnight or wanting to exchange numbers. They just want to bang one more famous motocross guy.

I swallow and focus on my next turn. I aim my cue and barely miss getting the ball in the hole. Dammit.

Tommy sinks the eight ball next and wins the game. One of his buddies offers to play him next, and I happily give over my pool stick. I need another beer.

I'm walking to the bar when I hear her voice.

"Can you idiots just *move*?"

I look over and find Bree giving a very pissed off look to two drunk guys who are dancing around like idiots. It takes me a second but I realize they're purposely blocking the bathroom door from her. I guess they think they're funny, but they're too drunk to realize they're just assholes.

"Get the hell out of the way," I say. The guys grimace at the sight of me, but they leave.

Bree's eyes widen and it kills me that she doesn't seem the least bit happy to see me right now.

"Can I buy you a drink?" I ask.

"I'm not old enough to drink," she says, putting a hand on the bathroom door.

"Wait, how old are you?"

"Twenty," she says, then she pushes open the door and slips inside. The women's bathroom is just one small room with a toilet and a sink, and I can see inside without being a creep about it.

Bree's foot keeps the door propped open to let in the light, because no one turned on the light in there. "Mia?" Bree says, leaning in. "You in here?"

She flips on the light, revealing a very drunk girl with dark brown hair who leans against the wall.

"Shit," Bree says, and then she lets the door close behind her.

I want to go in and help but it is the women's restroom, and I'm not exactly allowed in there.

I wait outside the door. I can hear Bree talking loudly to the girl, trying to get her to wake up or pay attention. After a few minutes, I knock.

"Need some help?"

"No," Bree calls back. "Go away."

But I can't leave. There is nothing in this bar that would be better than staying here and seeing Bree one more time.

A cloud of perfume appears next to me, followed by a girl with glassy eyes and an empty drink in her hand. "That's the girl's bathroom," she says, her voice slurred. "Boy's bathroom is over there."

"I know," I say.

She reaches out and grabs my crotch, which makes me freeze. "Let's get out of here," she says, giving me a lazy grin. "I give the best head you'll ever have."

I gently tug her hand off my jeans. "No, thanks."

She rolls her eyes. "Your loss," she sing-songs as she saunters away.

The bathroom door opens and Bree kicks it with her foot. She's got the girl's arm swung over her shoulder and she's attempting to half drag her out of the bathroom. Only this girl is much taller than Bree, and although she's half-conscious, she's not even attempting to walk on her own.

"Whoa," I say, catching the girl before she falls face first to the filthy floor. "Come here," I say. I put one arm under her back and bend down to grab under her knees and lift her off the ground. She folds into me, smelling like whiskey and cigar smoke.

Bree leads the way as I carry the woman outside and into the cool night air. "Just set her on the bench," Bree says, pointing.

I carefully fold the drunk girl onto the bench in as comfortable of a position as I can manage. Her eyes loll around and then she grins. "I'm freaking wasted," she says, giggling. Then she turns to the side and pukes all over the grass.

I jump back to avoid being hit with any of it.

"Thanks," Bree says. "I've got it from here."

"You sure?"

Bree's stern expression tells me she's never been more sure of anything in her life. "Yes. Please go."

CHAPTER 8

Bree

Why is he even here?

Zach Pena is the last person I care to see when I'm dragging my drunk cousin out of a bar. Although I'm grateful that *someone* was there to help me carry her out, I wish it wasn't him. It could have been anyone else and I'd have gratefully accepted their help. Why did fate give me *him*?

This is the worst I've ever seen Mia. She's been drinking ever since her boyfriend broke up with her about three months ago. She always calls me, drunk, from the bathroom of the bar. Sometimes she doesn't even make it to the bar, and she's just sitting in her parking spot at her apartment complex, falling over drunk off a cheap bottle of vodka.

It's getting worse, though. I wonder if I should tell my parents about this, or just keep trying to handle it myself. Mia has never been so drunk that I couldn't help her walk out to her car.

I sit next to her on the bench. She's half slumped over, but tries to push herself up into a sitting position. The air smells like puke, but throwing up seems to have sobered her a little bit. She brushes her messy hair out of her face and stares at me.

It takes a few seconds for her to register my face. "Bree!" she says, as if I just arrived and she hasn't seen me in months. Her face splits into a big grin. "I missed you."

"You're the one who called me over here," I say. "You're drunk. We need to get you home."

Behind us, country music blares through the bar, but it's real music from a famous artist. I guess that shitty cover band finally took a break and the bar put on some house music.

I brush Mia's hair behind her ears and take her face in my hands. "Look at me."

Her eyes are bloodshot and glassy, but she looks at me. "Where are your car keys?" I ask. I have to keep my voice calm and direct or she starts giggling or changing the subject. I've dealt with her enough times now to know what to do.

"I don't wanna go home," she slurs.

I roll my eyes. "We're not going home," I lie. "We just have to pick up a new outfit and then we'll come back."

Drunk people are stupid because they believe anything you say. Her face lights up. "Okay! Good idea!"

"So where are your keys?" I ask. "I'll drive us."

The bar is a mile away from my house, and since I don't want Mia leaving her car here overnight, I always just walk here and then drive her home in her own car. The walk from her apartments to my house is a little longer, but I can usually make it home in forty-five minutes. If my parents ever found out that

I'm walking on the back roads late at night, they'd murder me before someone else could.

Mia reaches into her pocket and pulls out a keychain. I take them and tuck them into my own pocket. "Okay, lct's go."

I stand up and hold out my hands to her. She's twenty-five years old and about a foot taller than me, but our whole lives have felt like I'm the older more responsible one. Mia reaches out for me, but she doesn't take my hands and stand up, like I'm hoping she will. Instead she starts wiggling her arms and swaying her hips although she's sitting, and I realize she's dancing to the new song that just came on.

"Mia, *dammit*!" I snap my fingers in front of her face, but it doesn't get her attention. This is so damn annoying. Maybe I should call my parents, even though it's late and they're both sleeping and we all have work tomorrow. Maybe I should just have them take care of it instead of it all falling to me.

I take a deep breath and let it out slowly. I try to remember the good times with my cousin and all the fun sleepovers we had as a kid. I love her, and she's just suffering right now.

"Come on," I say. I lean down and wrap my arms around her and pull her into a standing position. Then I put her arm over my shoulder and I wrap mine around her waist and try to pull her along. She's still shimmying to the music but she does walk with me toward her car.

I open the passenger door and she kind of falls into it, but at least she's in there. I pick up her feet and put them in the car and then close the door, not bothering with her seatbelt. We don't have to drive very far, and I'm just not in the mood to wrangle a seatbelt around her.

I get in her car and try to crank the engine, but it doesn't turn over. This old Honda Accord has seen better days, but I didn't think it would break down anytime soon. I try again, and again.

Then I notice the blinking red light on the dashboard. She's out of gas.

"Mia," I say, groaning in frustration.

The nearest gas station is entirely too far to walk to.

I look over at my cousin, and she's already asleep. She's even snoring softly, her head lolled to the side. I sit here a little while longer and try to think of a plan. I guess I could walk back to my house, borrow Mom's car, drive to the nearest gas station that's still open this late, and get gas and then bring it back here. I look over at Mia. Can I just leave her here sleeping? I could roll down the windows…

No, I can't. If I leave her here alone, drunk, and asleep, I'm just asking for one of those drunken men to stumble out here and take advantage of her. I couldn't live with myself if anything happened to her.

I lower my forehead to the steering wheel and close my eyes. What the hell am I going to do?

A tap on the window startles the hell out of me. I bolt upright and see Zach standing there, his knuckles pressed to the glass. He gives me a little wave.

"You okay?"

I am so close to telling him to piss off, but I'm also close to tears. As much as I don't want anything to do with this player, maybe he can help.

I open the door and get out of the car that's starting to smell like body odor, liquor, and puke.

"The car is out of gas," I say, staring at the car instead of Zach. "She must have driven here on fumes before she got too damn drunk to take care of herself."

I sigh.

"That's okay," Zach says. "I'll drive her home."

I shake my head. "I don't want to leave her car here. I just need gas for it."

He shrugs. "I'll get it towed back. Get some gas put in it, too."

I bite my lower lip. His offer is exactly what I need, but why did it have to come from him? And why is he even here? He should be off in big cities at fancy hotels hooking up with party girls. That's what his entire Instagram is about, and he seems really good at it.

He shouldn't be here, looking sexy as hell in the moonlight, that black t-shirt hugging all his muscles in all the right ways, making me want him like I've never wanted anyone else.

As much as I need his help, I can't stand the thought of being close to him for any longer. He makes my insides all warm and tingly, and his very presence is a constant reminder that I'll never get a guy as hot as him. I'm about to make up an excuse for why I don't need his help, but then he leaves.

No—he walks over to Mia's side of the car and opens the door and lifts her out of the seat effortlessly.

I follow him across the parking lot to a black Chevy truck because it's not like I have any choice now. He opens the back door and sets my cousin down in the backseat. She mumbles something but then settles down quietly.

God, I hope she doesn't puke in his truck.

"Get in," Zach says. He tosses me his keys. "Start the engine so ya'll can cool off. I'm gonna get some buddies to help me tow her car."

It's too late to refuse his help now. I get into his lifted truck and slide over the seat to start the engine.

This truck is massive and roomy, not at all like my dad's small pickup.

The leather seats smell amazing. I turn on the AC and then slide back over to the passenger seat which feels so far away from the driver's side. Good. I need as much space as I can get between Zach and me.

A few minutes later, Zach returns and gets in the truck.

"Her name's Mia, right?" he asks.

I nod. "Mia Grayson."

"Cool," he says. "My buddy Tommy said he knows her and he'll tow her car back home tonight and put some gas in it."

"You know little Tom?" I ask.

He grins. "Yep. He's a good guy. You can trust him with her car."

I nod. "I know."

"Westfall Apartments?" he asks.

I guess little Tom told him that information, too. I nod and he starts driving there.

My cousin is passed out in the back seat, and although the radio plays softly in the background, it feels unbearably quiet in here. I want to talk to him—hell, who am I kidding—I want to do *way more* than talk to him. But my body freezes up and I can't seem to do anything but sit here, quietly admiring his good looks while he drives.

The trip is way too short and soon we're here. I direct him to her building and he parks right in front of it. Then he carries my cousin all the way to her front door, up two flights of stairs.

I'm about as turned on as you can get while I watch him do all of this work without even getting winded. If he's strong enough to carry a girl up two flights of stairs, what could he do in bed?

Stop it, Bree. Stop thinking about him like that.

I unlock her door and we tuck Mia into bed. I put a glass of water and two Aspirin on her nightstand and then we leave her to sleep off the booze.

"Thank you," I say as we descend the stairs together.

"It's not a problem."

We reach the bottom stair and Zach bumps into me with his arm. When I look at him, he's giving me a playful grin. "Thanks for letting me help you."

I look away. "It's not like I had a choice."

"You did. You could have told me to piss off again."

"I've never told you to piss off," I say.

He chuckles. "Not in those exact words, but—the implication was there."

He's being playful and I can't help but smile. He opens the truck door for me and I climb inside. Sitting in the passenger seat, I'm about eye level with him. He looks like he wants to say something, but instead he winks and then closes the door.

It's the sexiest wink in the history of the world.

We drive in silence from Mia's apartment to the track. I don't have to tell him where I live, so I guess he already knows. That means he figured out who I am. I wonder if he remembers me from way back when.

I think about asking, but I can't. It's too hard to talk around him. He smells just like his bedroom did, and it's a struggle to sit here and act normal when I'd rather close my eyes and breathe in the sexy scent of his cologne until my ovaries burst. Everything about him is sexy as hell.

This is torture. Being so close to a guy I can never have.

Sure, I bet he'd sleep with me because he's a man whore. But I'm not that type of girl. Part of me wishes I was that type of girl. Then I could have him and finally know if my daydreams were right about what it would be like to sleep with him.

I have to take a deep breath to calm myself down.

Zach pulls into the side driveway that leads to our house. You can also get there from the track's main entrance but since it's the middle of the night, the track is closed and so is the large gate on the main entrance.

He turns off his headlights and coasts to a stop.

"You're more fun to hang out with than my buddies," he says.

I roll my eyes. "We didn't even talk much."

"And yet you're still better company," he says with a grin. "Maybe it's because you're much prettier and smell a hell of a lot better than my friends."

I'm glad it's dark in here and he can't see me blush. I have no idea what comes over me right now, but my insides are throbbing with heat and desire. Zach will probably go back to Nashville any day now and I'll be all out of chances to do something I've only ever fantasized about.

I can't believe I'm going to do this… I look him dead in the eyes, and I say, "Want to come inside?"

CHAPTER 9

ZACH

There are times in a man's life where he must choose between what he *should* do and what he *wants* to do. I've made a lot of mistakes in my life, and I'm still paying for some of them. You think I would have learned my lesson by now. And yet, here I am, staring into Bree's dark brown eyes as she watches me eagerly from the passenger side of my truck, and I know I am about to make another mistake. She's spent days avoiding me and yet, in a complete one-eighty, she just invited me to come inside.

I think she's making a mistake too.

"Yeah," I say, shutting off the truck. I pull out my keys and step outside before she can change her mind.

I watch her bite her bottom lip as she slowly walks up to the front porch of her trailer. I follow quietly, admiring her backside under the glow of the moonlight. She's wearing black leggings and a purple tank top that shows off her bikini tan line on her shoulders. I want to trace that tan line with my tongue.

That'll be the first thing I do.

At the front door, Bree turns around to face me. The wooden porch is small and the planks creak under my weight. I give her a little smile, hoping she's not about to change her mind.

"My parents are home," she says in a whisper. "So be quiet."

I nod once, not taking my gaze off hers. Maybe it's the moonlight, or all my pent up sexual energy, but she's gorgeous as hell right now and it's turning me on.

She opens the front door and puts her finger to her lips, reminding me to be quiet. We enter into a dark living room and Bree reaches for my hand. Her skin is soft and warm and my dick hardens just thinking about having those hands holding onto me in other ways.

She leads me down a narrow hallway and into a bedroom at the very end of the trailer. Once we're inside, she drops my hand and my chest aches because of it. She closes the bedroom door and then turns on a small lamp in the corner. The room lights up with a soft yellow glow and I make a point of looking around the tiny bedroom.

She has a larger bed than I do, and it's made up with a black comforter that has white roses printed on it. There's a mountain of pillows all arranged in a neat order. Her furniture is black and the décor seems to be purposely black and white. She has a large bookshelf against one wall, next to her desk with a laptop on it. Everything is neat and tidy and it confirms that she's exactly the kind of girl I thought she was.

A girl that's too good for me.

"Someone likes books," I say, giving her a playful grin.

"Books are the best." She puts her hands on her hips as if challenging me to disagree.

I shrug. "Books are okay."

She rolls her eyes and glances at her bookshelf. "Most of those are from college. Only that small collection on the top shelf are the books I actually enjoy reading."

"What'd you study in college?" I ask. I'd just like to point out that I'm trying very hard here. Trying to be friendly and polite, instead of following my true desires of throwing her on the bed and having my way with her.

She says something and—dammit—I don't even hear it. I'm staring at her lips, how they're pouty and perfect and how I only just now realized that the front of her is just as sexy as the back of her. Bree Grayson is the whole package.

I shove my hands in my pockets in an attempt to hide what I've got going on here. I don't want her to see my massive erection and change her mind about inviting me inside. Or maybe I do. I don't even know what I want right now.

I know that I want her so bad, but that taking her would be the very opposite of what I came to Hopewell to do this summer. I should turn right around and leave and keep the promise I made to myself. But of course, I don't do that.

"Well?" Bree says. Her hands are on her hips and she's looking at me from across the room.

Shit, I have no idea what she was talking about. "Well," I say back to her, tilting my head a little like I'm just playing with her. Hopefully she won't realize that I wasn't listening to whatever she'd said because I was too busy checking her out.

"Come on, Zach," she says. Her shoulders fall and she looks so vulnerable right now. "Don't make me do it."

"Make you do what?" I ask.

Her eyes flash at me for a second, like she thinks I'm a total idiot. "You know why I invited over here," she says, somewhat sheepishly. "Don't make me make the first move. I mean, that's kind of *your* specialty, right?"

Oh *shit*.

I swallow. Her words are music to my ears. My heartbeat quickens. "Are you sure?"

She leans over and twists the lock on the doorknob. "I'm sure."

I wet my lips with the anticipation of kissing her, and I cross the room in two strides. Now we're closer than we ever have been, and she smells like an angel. She looks like one too, with those big innocent eyes staring up at me expectantly.

My heart thunders in my chest. I've never felt this way before. Usually the first kiss is the easiest part, a very forgettable part, of hooking up. But this feels different. I reach out and place my hands on her hips. She inches forward, her toes curling on the carpet. I gaze into her eyes and then I can't take it anymore. I lower my lips to hers.

She kisses me back with an eagerness I didn't quite expect. Soon, her hands are moving up my back and I'm pulling her closer, sliding my tongue between her lips. She gasps as I rock her hips against mine, then her hands tangle in my hair as she kisses me deeper.

My hands roam her body, over the soft flimsy fabric of those black leggings and back up to her breasts. My pants tighten even more when I realize she's not wearing a bra. There's just one thin layer of clothing separating me from her body. I trail kisses from her ear down her neck, reveling in the way she grips me tighter with each one. I kiss her collarbone and then slide my tongue up to just behind her ear. I breathe out softly and feel her skin turn to gooseflesh beneath my lips.

"Still time to back out," I whisper against her ear.

She shakes her head. "Not happening."

I scoop her up and place her on the bed, right on top of all the decorative pillows. Her hair cascades all around her, making her even more beautiful. Her eyes sparkle even in the dim lighting. I lower myself on top of her and kiss her softly. She tugs at my shirt, and I sit up and let her take it off. I want her clothing gone too, but even in the heat of passion something is telling me to take it slow. Girls like Bree deserve to be treated like the queen that they are.

Her gaze roams down my chest, making me extra appreciative of all the working out I did this week.

She puts her hands on my shoulders and leans up, kissing my neck.

I take a ragged breath, closing my eyes as her tongue flicks across my collarbone.

Bree is not like the other girls I hook up with. She's special. She'll be hurt if I hook up with her and then leave, and that's exactly what I'm going to do. After the summer is over, I'm gone.

"I don't think we should do this," I whisper, even though it kills me to say it.

Her eyebrows furrow. "Why not?" Her hand slides from my chest to my waistband and I know exactly what she's hinting.

I'm going to have the worst case of blue balls on the drive home, but I steel myself and do what I need to do. "Sorry," I say, bending down to kiss those perfect lips again. I want to explain how badly I want her. But I can't lead her on. She's too good of a girl for me and I can't hurt her any more than I probably already have. "Not tonight."

Her frown fades away and she nods once. "You're right," she says. She pushes at my chest and I climb off of her. She takes my shirt off the floor and hands it to me. "This can't happen again."

CHAPTER 10

Bree

I yawn, and it's that kind of huge yawn that you can't stop no matter how hard you try. I'm in the registration tower and the races start soon. I finally finished hanging all the stupid plastic flags around the track, and I was lucky enough to avoid seeing a particular guy I didn't want to see.

I'm about to reach for a bottled water from the fridge, but I yawn again and decide to make some coffee instead. Who cares if it's five in the afternoon? Coffee is the only thing that will save me besides a nap, and I can't exactly take a nap right now.

I'm exhausted and humiliated and just mad at myself. I won't say that I'm regretful, because being with Zach was all kinds of things I can't even describe because I don't know words strong enough to describe something so magical. It was also something I'll always remember. But I'm not too thrilled with the way it happened.

And who I was with.

Ugh, I'm such an idiot.

Why did I invite him inside?

Why did I flirt and kiss and —*heavily* make out with him?

I knew it was a bad idea from the moment I climbed into his truck, but something took over me when I saw his cute grin and the way he looks at me with those eyes. When he parked in front of my house, the very idea of walking into my house and letting him drive away was too much to handle. I felt suffocated. Like I had to have him. Like I *needed* to kiss him. I had to scratch that itch that's been bugging me since I first laid eyes on him.

And man, was it worth it.

Until he decided he didn't want to take things further. How am I supposed to handle that? I mean what kind of guy *doesn't* want to take things further? Sure, I was nervous and probably wouldn't even be good at it, but I wanted to return the favor. And he just shot me down. It doesn't make any sense.

I had tried acting like it was no big deal, like I totally agreed with him, but of course it was a big deal.

And because of the way things ended last night, I'd stayed up way too late. I laid in bed staring at the dark ceiling, thinking over all the reasons why Zach wouldn't want me. I replayed every second of our time together, relived every delicious kiss, and I still didn't figure out why he wouldn't want me. As I had watched him walk out my front door, I'd secretly been hoping he would turn around, stop, and ask for my phone number. Ask for a date. *Anything*. But he didn't do any of that.

I didn't even fall asleep until nine in the morning, and then Mama woke me up at noon saying they needed me at the track.

I thought about faking sick (although sleep deprivation is kind of a sickness, right?) to skip work today, but I need the money. I also don't want to let Mrs. Sam down since she depends on me so much.

I get paid a lot of money to hang out at the track and wave the yellow flag during the races. So for that reason, I'm here today. I'm doing it for the money.

But no amount of money will ever make me clean Zach's house again. Mama can do that one on her own.

I tap my foot while the coffee maker gurgles and makes my coffee. Mrs. Sam slips into the building, her forehead glistening with sweat. "Girl how can you drink coffee when it's hot as hell outside?" she says.

I yawn in reply. She rolls her eyes. "Whatever floats your boat."

I drink my coffee inside because it is too hot to drink it outside. I down it as quickly as possible and then grab a bottle of water to take outside with me.

There's no doubt I'll see Zach tonight since he signed up for tonight's race. But he's obviously trying to avoid me as much as I'm trying to avoid him because he signed up online.

I grab my yellow flag from a bin of them and walk out onto the track. Flaggers have an important role to play during a race. There's about ten of us, and we all stand on separate parts of the track, just off to the side where we won't get run over.

If a racer crashes during the race, we run over to him and wave the yellow flag to warn the rest of the racers that someone fell down. When the yellow flag is out, racers have to slow down and aren't allowed to pass each other until they're out of the area. This makes sure no one falls over and then gets crushed by a speeding bike.

Sometimes I can stand here all day long and no one falls over on my part of the track. But other days I'll be running back and forth constantly. Today, I'm at a soft corner part of the track that doesn't get much action. Good. I'm too exhausted to think right now.

I sit on a bale of hay that lines the track. I purposely didn't walk around today, so I have no idea where Zach is parked, and I like it that way. I don't need the temptation of trying to find him in the crowd of people.

The races begin, and I'm so tired I can barely function. One little kid falls over in my turn and rush over and wave the flag while he picks up his bike and gets it started again. He zooms off and I go back to my hay bale. Normally, I stand the whole time, but I'm just not having it today.

I focus on the races, watching the bikes and the counting them as they go past. Normally, I don't pay much attention, but right now I need anything to keep my mind off Zach.

The last thing I need is to remember the feel of his hand sliding down my leg...

Yeah, I can't think of that right now.

The sun sets and the air cools off. Most of the races are finished by now, but there's still a few left. I dread the final race, because Zach looks sexy as hell on a dirt bike. I promise myself I won't watch him, but it doesn't work. He's too gorgeous to miss. Too skilled on a bike to look away.

Zach zooms by in the lead on the very first lap. His head is down, his gaze focused solely on the track in front of him. Good. I don't want him to see me anyhow.

The overhead lights are bright and harsh, illuminating the track now that it's almost midnight. I've been awake for so long I feel like I'm going to pass out.

Zach makes another lap, and then another. The thunder of engines trail behind him as all the other guys scramble for second place. That's the best that they can get, because Zach is so far ahead that no one can catch up.

He flies over the finish line, and I'm so unbelievably grateful that the races are over. I'm going straight to bed, dirty and covered in sweat. I can shower in the morning. But for now, all I want, is sleep.

I drop my yellow flag off and then collect my money for the day. Mrs. Sam pays us in cash and I've just earned an easy $200.

I pocket the money and walk away quickly. Zach will be here any second to collect his winnings and I don't want to run into him. I can't possibly face the guy who gave me the hottest night of my life and then decided he wanted nothing more to do with me.

I walk away from the crowd, toward my house. My eyes are heavy and all I'm thinking about is falling into bed.

But then I pass a familiar black truck and my stomach tightens.

There he is. Shirtless and covered in a fine layer of sweat that makes him glisten like a Greek god. At least a dozen people are crowded around him, all trying to talk to the famous Zach Pena.

Two girls rush up and hold out their phones for a selfie with him. He throws his arms around their shoulders and smiles brightly.

That smile kills me.

That smile is what made me invite him into my bedroom. It's what made me kiss him. What made me trust him with my body.

And then last night, when it was all over, he wasn't smiling at all.

He looked like he regretted everything.

Well, I hope those girls are good enough to make him happy, because clearly I'm not.

CHAPTER 11

ZACH

Another week goes by and I am no better off than I was the moment Bree kicked me out of her house. My days are spent working out and riding. My nights are spent tuning up my dirt bike and watching TV with Mom and then getting a good night's sleep. It's like I'm twelve years old again.

I don't go out, even though Tommy asks me once a day if I want to get a beer. After that night with Bree, I haven't done anything. I'm not sure if I'm sulking because my ego is crushed, or if I'm just really throwing myself into my goal of focusing on motocross this summer. I tell myself it's the second one.

Eventually, the days pass and it's Friday again. Another race day. Another chance to win five hundred dollars.

And another chance to see Bree.

I didn't see her at all last week, although that's partially my own fault. I didn't leave my truck except to ride. I didn't want to see her. It was too fresh, too raw.

We'd had an amazing time together, and I didn't want it to end. But then it did. Abruptly, and painfully. Maybe I scared her by not letting her return the favor. I had just been so shocked by her admission that no one had ever pleased her the way I did that I felt guilty. Like I was taking advantage of her.

And I still feel that way, but it hasn't helped me get over her. I can't stop thinking about her lips on mine. The smell of her shampoo, the feel of her skin.

I should either sleep with her or make her hate me. Either way, I need to get this girl out of my system.

I skip practice this morning. I'm fitter than ever, and I don't need an extra hour on the track to know I'll easily win the race today. I want to see her again, so I park right up close to the registration building. She'll have to walk by my truck to get anywhere and I'll be there, looking for her.

Mrs. Sam sits behind the registration counter. I hand over my money and she greets me with a big smile. "Boy, you're bringing in so many people by racing here. Our numbers have doubled."

I crack a grin. "I'm glad I'm helping out."

"I got you signed up," she says after I hand back the tablet. "Have a good race."

I linger for a moment and then decide to just go for it. "Hey, Mrs. Sam? Do you know where Bree is?"

My ears feel hot and for a second I worry that she'll know exactly why I'm asking. Mrs. Sam is no doubt protective over Bree since she's known her for so long. But I guess I'm not wearing my emotions too plainly on my sleeve because she just shrugs.

"She's flagging today. You might find her on the track since the first race is about to start."

I thank her and then check the race schedule. There are only twenty races tonight, which is a little fewer than usual. That means the night will be over quicker, and my time for finding Bree and making her like me is already running out.

On the short walk from registration to the bleachers, I get stopped five times. I take five pictures with people and answer about a million questions. Two girls flirt with me and I'm pretty sure one of them is extremely under age. Not happening.

I maintain my smiles and good attitude because of my promise to my fans, but it's annoying as hell right now. I just need to get up the bleachers so I can get a good view of the track and find her.

Finally, I make it to the top and gaze out over the track. It's a large trail that meanders through the natural sloping terrain. You can see most of it from up here, but not all.

The first race begins and it's a bunch of little kids on tiny bikes. The motors are so small it sounds like a swarm of mosquitos are flying around.

Eventually, I find a tiny figure on the track. She has long dark hair and is holding a yellow flag. The rest of the flaggers look too tall or short or manly to be Bree. This one must be her, even though she's so far away I can barely tell.

I jog down the bleachers and make my way toward her. But it's a long walk, and hopping over the fcncc during a race isn't exactly allowed. I look around and realize I'll have to take the long way—walking all the way around the outside of the track until I get to her.

But then I see one of the race dads standing at his truck, pouring gas into his kid's bike. I recognize him because he and his son have stopped to talk to me a few times. His son thinks I'm the greatest rider of all time.

"Hello," I say, walking up to the guy. "How are you doing?"

"Hi, Zach! I'm doing just fine. What about you?"

"I'm ready to ride," I say with a smile. "Sucks that my race is the last one of the night."

"That's for sure," he says.

If this were a national race and I was with Team Loco, I'd have no problem asking for a favor. But since

I'm just Zach Pena right now—not a famous Team Loco racer—it's a little harder.

"Hey, would you mind if I borrowed your four wheeler for a bit?"

"Oh sure man," he says eagerly, setting the gas can back on the ground. "You can use it anytime."

I've seen this look on so many people before. They're eager to be friends with the mildly famous guy. Girls do it, guys do it, and parents do it. I'll admit, this past year when I was flying from city to city racing with the big names and reaping the rewards of fame, I let it go to my head a bit.

And then I met a girl who doesn't give a shit about that. And now I just feel guilty using my fame like this. Would this guy have loaned his four wheeler to anyone else? Probably not.

I ride the four wheeler through the parking lot and around the back of the track. It's much quicker than walking, and soon I can see Bree standing at a corner turn of the track, yellow flag in her hand.

I roll up next to her and cut the motor. She turns around, not looking at all surprised until she sees it's me on the four wheeler.

"Hey there," I say. I stay seated.

Her hair is in a low ponytail and she's wearing a red Hopewell MX shirt over a pair of cut off shorts and some red Converse. I absolutely love how she looks like summer. Casual and carefree and gorgeous. She doesn't wear a pound of makeup or clothes that look like they belong in a club instead of outside in the dirt.

Bree Grayson would be the perfect motocross girlfriend. She knows the sport and isn't some hoe who's just trying to latch on to anyone famous.

She lifts an eyebrow. "You're not supposed to be here. You're not an employee."

"I'm Zach Pena," I say, giving her a wink. "I can do whatever I want."

She rolls her eyes. "No you can't."

I climb off the four wheeler and look around. "I don't see anyone coming to stop me."

She pulls a small black radio off her hip and holds it up to her mouth. "Hey Dad? Can you send security over here to escort Zach Pena off the premises?"

"Oh shit," I say, holding out my hands. "I'm sorry. I'll leave."

She grins and puts the radio back on her hip. "I didn't push the button," she says, giving me mischievous look. "But I do have ways to stop you from breaking the track rules."

"Fair enough," I say. "I'll leave... but only if you want me to."

Her eyes meet mine and I immediately feel the pull of desire between us. I know it can't just be one-sided. She has to feel it, too. She takes a step backward and looks down at her flag.

"It doesn't matter what I want. You're not supposed to be out here. It's a safety violation."

"That means you want me to stay?" I say, giving her a flirty look. This look does not fail me with other girls, and it doesn't fail me with Bree. She smiles a little even though she's trying not to.

She waves her hand at me in a shooing motion. "Just go away. Go mess with some other girl."

"Why?" I ask. "I want to mess with you."

Her cheeks get a little pink and it's all the encouragement I need to keep going. "So what's stopping you? You gotta boyfriend?"

"No," she says with a wry snort.

"Husband?" I say. "Fiancé?"

"Definitely not."

"So what is it?" I ask, playfully poking her in the arm. "Why did you let me in and then kick me out?"

She holds up a finger. "That was a mistake. A *one time* mistake. We can be casual—super casual—friends, but that's it."

Her words stab me right through the heart. The F word is not okay with me right now. I don't want to be *friends* with this girl.

A roar of bikes fills the air and three racers fly around the track. The fourth one hits the turn too quickly, and his tire hops over a rut in the dirt. He face plants. The kid is probably about ten years old and his bike is now partially stuck in the dirt. He scrambles to his feet and reaches for his bike, but it's too heavy.

I run toward him and pull the bike out of the dirt. I hold it out for him and he shakes his head.

"I can't start it without my dad's help," he says, his voice muffled from his helmet. Two more bikes zoom past us. I climb on the bike and kickstart it for him, revving the engine as I hold the bike out. He's short but he scrambles on it.

"Thank you!" he calls out as he shifts into gear and takes off again.

I get out of the way while a few more bikes barrel through the rutted dirt and then I jog back over to Bree, who is putting her yellow flag back down.

"What if I don't want to be friends?" I say, not willing to let a little distraction stop our conversation.

She stares at me for a long moment. "Why me?" she asks. "Is it because I don't throw myself at you like every other girl out here? Do you just need to keep your ego in check? Are you trying to win some bet that you can sleep with every chick in Hopewell? I told you to go away and you didn't, so why me, Zach?"

"Because you're beautiful," I say. The words tumble out before I can think of a better way to say them. "You're the most beautiful girl I've ever seen. You're smart and kind and you work hard and don't expect things to be given to you. You're the kind of person I want to be. You call me on my bullshit and you don't give me a free pass because I used to be famous."

"You're still famous," she mutters.

Our eyes meet and she looks down at her shoes.

"Not really," I say. "Not in the way that matters, at least. But I don't care about the fame when I'm around you. When I'm around you, I just want more time with you. And no, it's not just because you keep turning me down." I take a deep breath. "Although, I do wish you'd stop doing that…"

A tiny smile appears on her face. Her eyes flit upward to mine, and her bottom lip tucks under her teeth.

My heart feels all fluttery and I hold my breath in anticipation of what she'll say next. Because I think, maybe, just maybe, I might have won her over.

CHAPTER 12

Bree

I know I'm going to smile. I know I'm going to forgive him for the weirdness of last Friday night and I know I'll agree to see him again if he ever asks.

But I make him wait a few moments before I say anything.

The sun is shining overhead and bikes are rumbling past us with each lap. I try not to think about how sexy it was that Zach ran out and started that bike for the kid who fell over.

Finally, after a little while, I shrug. "I guess we can hang out."

"After the races," Zach says, and I don't know if it's a question or if he's telling me the future. "I'll shower and then come by your house and pick you up."

"Where will we go that late on a Friday night?" I ask. "You know I'm not old enough to go to a bar."

He shakes his head. "Bars aren't fun. I'll take you somewhere fun."

And then, with a grin that could melt steel, Zach gets back on the four wheeler he rode up on and drives away, leaving me breathless and unable to focus on the races.

What on earth did I just agree to? Is it a date?

Are we just going to hook up again?

The thought of kissing him again sends a shiver of excitement through my toes. After promising myself I wouldn't let that player get anywhere near me again, here I am practically salivating at the idea of making out with him.

This can't be good.

Somehow I manage to make it through the rest of the races, and soon the sun has set and the bright stadium lights overhead light up the track. The cash class lines up at the gate, and then the final race of the night begins.

I stand off to the side of the track, my yellow flag in my hand. Zach is in the lead as he soars across the track. Unlike last week, he knows exactly where I'm standing. When he reaches the turn next to me, I see his helmet lift up a little. He lets go of the throttle and points at me, just for a second, and then he speeds off again.

I don't know why, but it's the hottest thing ever. I feel floaty for the rest of the race. There are girls in the bleachers and standing behind the fence watching him race, wishing he was their man. There are no doubt tons of girls waiting for the race to be over so they can go get a picture with him or ask for his autograph.

And out of all those girls, he just pointed at me.

When the checkered flag flies and Zach does a no-handed trick jump over the finish line, I can't stop the butterflies in my stomach from freaking out. He's going to go home and shower and then pick me up. I don't know how long he plans on taking, but I can't risk being sweaty from twelve hours in the sun when he shows up.

I rush back to the building, drop off my flag, grab my day's earnings from Mrs. Sam, and then jog all the way home.

Inside, Mama is listening to music and folding laundry. I don't say anything to her because then she might ask what I'm up to. I don't want to lie to Mama, and I don't want to tell the truth.

I shower quickly and fix my hair, brushing out the tangles from it being in a ponytail all day. I stand in my closet and stare at it for entirely too long, finally deciding on a black cotton dress I got from Forever 21. It's simple and soft, with spaghetti straps that crisscross down my back.

I wear a pair of black flip-flops and then put on some mascara and lip gloss. I don't look like the other girls at the track, but it's the best I can do.

When Zach's headlights blast across my bedroom window, I rush out and grab my keys. "I'm heading out with friends," I call out as casually as possible. Dad is still at the track helping clean up, and Mama barely looks up from the laundry.

"Have fun," she says.

I step outside before Zach can make it to the front door. I've never been embarrassed about the people I hang out with before, but there's something about Zach. I guess I don't want my parents knowing that I'm hanging out with such a womanizer. They'll think I'm smarter than this.

I used to think I was smarter than this, but then Zach came into my life and here I am, walking right up to him as if I'm eagerly waiting to get my heart broken.

I swallow the lump in my throat as the reality of this situation hits me like a brick to the face. What even am I doing?

This is stupid! He's a player and I'm better than this.

"You look amazing," Zach says, giving me that grin. He's halfway from his truck to my front door and I'm still standing on the porch having an attack of conscience. I should be smart and tell him to go away.

But another part of me decides that I'm a grown woman and I can choose to be a player just like Zach. I can hang out with him all I want – no strings attached.

"You look *okay*," I say with a smirk.

His grin widens. "Well compared to you, I'm a disgusting troll."

Hardly.

Zach walks over to the passenger side and opens the door for me. Just being in his truck again reminds me of last weekend. I take a slow, deep breath as he walks over to the driver's side. I tell myself to stay cool. Keep calm. You can be a player too, Bree.

Zach's truck is clean and smells like leather and man. I don't talk much on the drive because I'm not sure what to say. Even if I'm trying to be this amazing casual girl, I still feel nerdy inside.

Zach talks a little about the races, but the few moments of silence aren't awkward with him.

"So where are we going?" I ask when we turn onto a county road.

He rolls down the windows with the touch of a button and the cool night air flows into the truck. "We're here."

I look out my window and almost laugh. I can't believe I didn't think of it earlier.

The lake.

Lake Hopewell was my favorite place in the world before I started college. I used to come out here every weekend with my friends. In the summer we'd go swimming and in the winter we'd build a bonfire and roast marshmallows. But once college classes started, I got too busy to bother with silly things like that. I wonder if my friends still come to the lake, or if they gave up on having fun when I ditched them two years ago.

"Good choice," I say, gazing out at the view. The moonlight sparkles on the water. It's just after eleven at night, which isn't too late for a Friday but the place is empty. I'm happy for the privacy because something tells me that being out in public with Zach would be more like being a part of his fan club.

And tonight, I want him all to myself.

We park on the sand and I step out of the truck and inhale a deep breath of fresh air. Zach parked so that the back of his truck was facing the water, and he lets down the tailgate.

"Not yet," Zach says when I go to sit on it. He takes something from the backseat—a blanket—and then spreads it out on the metal. "I don't want your dress to get dirt on it," he says.

We sit on the blanket, our feet dangling off the tailgate. A cool breeze ripples over the water and through the trees beyond, and the sounds of nature are the only thing in the air for a short while.

Zach leans back on his hands and looks over at me. "Tell me something good," he says.

I look up at the sky, wondering if this is a test to see how clever or cool I am. What do the other girls say when he asks them that question? Or does he even talk with other girls? There's probably just a lot of sloppy kissing and hooking up going on with most of the girls he's with.

I look over at him, surprised to see that he's still watching me.

I say the first thing I can think of. "I'm bilingual."

"Impressive," he says. "I'm monolingual."

I laugh. "Maybe I'll teach you Spanish sometime."

There's a kindness in his eyes and it makes me uneasy. Like if I look into them too long I might fall right on in and never be able to escape the pull of Zach Pena.

I run my hands down my dress, flattening it out over my thighs. "Now you tell me something cool."

"You are the only cool thing I know right now," he says without any hesitation.

I roll my eyes. "Firstly, I'm not cool. And secondly, you know lots of cool things."

"Cool is in the eye of the beholder," he says. "And lately my whole life has been shit."

I lift an eyebrow. "How?"

He exhales. "I'm stuck in Hopewell all summer."

"Stuck?" I ask.

He nods. "Stuck. I'm not here by choice. I'm here because I screwed up."

I wait for him to continue. He glances at me and then looks back out at the water. "I didn't qualify for the summer circuit with Team Loco. I had to give up my apartment and move in with my mom like a complete failure."

"You're off Team Loco?" I ask, unable to hide my shock.

He shakes his head. "Not officially. If I don't qualify for the fall season then yeah, I'll be screwed. Right now I'm just—temporarily not good enough."

"Wow," I say. "That sucks."

"There's no one to blame but myself. I screwed up, I slacked off and partied too hard and it cost me a spot on the lineup." He runs his hands through his hair. I can feel the pain he feels, the bitter disappointment of not being good enough.

I've felt that way for weeks now. Ever since I graduated.

Zach's tongue flicks across his bottom lip while he watches the water. I know this is a serious moment, so I try not to picture running my tongue over his. He looks at me and I blush, hoping he can't read my thoughts.

"But I promised myself I'd fix this. I'm spending all summer working out and practicing so that when the fall qualifiers come around, I'll make it. I'm not giving up my shot at being pro so soon. I deserve to be on the team, and I'll prove it."

"That's good," I say. "You've been working your ass off lately."

He grins. "How do you know that?"

I blush even harder, but luckily the moonlight hides my embarrassment. "I live on the track," I say. "I see everything."

He smiles and looks back at the lake. "I haven't exactly told anyone else about my epic failure so..."

I mimic zipping my lips closed. "Your secret is safe with me."

"Thanks," he says, and there's so much gratitude and sadness in his voice that I feel suddenly bad for him. Despite what it might look like from the outside, he's not having the best summer either.

I slide off the tailgate and give him a mischievous smile. "I know exactly what you need," I say.

He looks on with interest. "What's that?"

I'm feeling bold, and I've done this a thousand times with my friends but never with a guy I liked. Still, it's now or never, and I am determined to cheer him up.

I reach for the hem of my dress and pull it up over my head. I'm wearing a matching black bra and panties, which is basically a bathing suit.

Zach's eyes widen and I toss my dress in his face. "Let's go swimming," I say.

"I thought you were going to say something else," he mutters as he places my dress on the blanket. "But this is good, too."

He shrugs out of his jeans and pulls off his shirt. I turn toward the water, not wanting to look at his sculpted chest too long because it'll make me weak and then I won't be able to walk.

My toes sink into the sand as I run into the water. It's still warm from the hot summer day and I run out full force until the water is up to my thighs, and then I sink into it.

Zach is right behind me, wearing a tight pair of boxer briefs that leave very, *very* little to the imagination.

I swim out until my feet barely touch the bottom. Zach joins me, his skin sparkling in the glow of the moonlight.

"The water feels great," he says.

I hold up my fingers to the water and flick some of it on his face.

He laughs and splashes me back. For a while, we play around like kids, squealing and splashing each other. Finally I hold up my hands in surrender.

"I give up!" I say. "My mouth tastes like lake."

"I bet it tastes better than that," Zach says.

He moves closer to me. He looks gorgeous with wet hair and water drops rolling down his muscular shoulders. I probably look like a mess, my hair all stringy and gross, but the way Zach looks at me says he doesn't see any of that.

He closes the distance between us and soon we're two heads floating in the water just inches apart. I reach out for him and grab his shoulders. My toes lift off the bottom of the lake as he pulls me closer. His hands slide over my butt and down my legs as he guides me to where my legs are wrapped around him. I hook my ankles together around his back and stare into his eyes.

His strong hands hold onto my sides, not letting me float away. I can feel his erection pushing against the fabric of his boxers, pressing into my abdomen.

Zach's eyes stare into mine, and there's something new in the feeling it gives me. We seem closer now that he's shared some of his life with me. It feels better this time.

My whole body aches to be joined with his, but I'll settle for a kiss first.

"Come here," Zach whispers.

I lean forward and press my lips to his, giving both of us exactly what we want.

CHAPTER 13

ZACH

I wake up to the sunlight pouring into my room. My first thoughts are a confused mess because it's never sunny when I wake up. I've been up at six a.m. every day so I can work out.

But as I stretch and yawn and roll over in this tiny ass bed, it all makes sense. I turned off my 6 a.m. alarm last night because I'd gotten home just three hours before that.

I spent all weekend with Bree. Each night we stayed out later than the night before. I block the sunlight from my eyes with my arm and yawn again as memories of last night come back to me. We'd gone into town to see a movie. We sat in the back row. This theater recently renovated all of the seats and now instead of some crappy fold down chair, they all have plush leather recliners that lean way back. About fifteen minutes into the film, I'd pulled her into my lap. We stayed like that for the whole movie, Bree cuddled in my lap, resting her head on my chest, her knees bent over the armrest while her feet hovered over her abandoned chair.

Then I'd driven her home and kissed her goodbye on the front porch. It was the best night of my life. We didn't hook up. We even kept our clothes on. This is a first for me.

Dating a girl without sex, without taking it farther just because I want to.

And trust me, I want to. But Bree is special. I don't mind just spending time with her, in fact I crave it. All we've done this weekend is hold hands and kiss and talk about our lives. And yet somehow, this time with Bree is better than any time I've ever spent hooking up with some girl.

I sit up in bed with a big ass grin on my face, and I'm pretty sure you could offer me a million dollars to stop smiling, and I wouldn't be able to. This girl has a hold on me. This girl is beautiful and sweet and I think she's falling for me the way I'm falling for her.

Thoughts I don't want to think about invade my subconscious. Like how she's too good for me. How I'm in no place to start dating a girl. How this will only end in a messed up heartache because I don't even know *how* to date a girl. I just know how to hook up with girls I'll never have to see again.

I shove the thoughts away. Maybe I'm just a shit person, too selfish for my own good, but I want to keep seeing her. I *need* to keep seeing her. Even though the end of the summer will mean the end of us.

Screw it, I don't care.

This girl gives me life. Happiness. Maybe I didn't need to come back to Hopewell to get back in shape for racing. Maybe I was destined to meet her. Maybe I just needed someone to ground me back to earth and show me what it feels like to be loyal to someone.

After all, being loyal is one skill I need to practice. Not strength training, or agility, or endurance on a dirt bike. I'm already great at that. I need loyalty. To my bike, to my team, to my sport. I need to stop the party life and settle down and focus on the one thing that matters: motocross.

I pull on a T-shirt as I try to rationalize my feelings for Bree. Maybe it'll all work out. Maybe she'll have fun hanging with me this summer and then we'll just go our separate ways and it'll be fine.

Mom is cooking something that smells amazing when I leave my bedroom. "What are you cooking?" I ask. "I'm starving."

"Pulled pork sandwiches," Mom says. She lifts the lid of her crockpot and reaches for a fork.

"For breakfast?" I ask.

She snorts. "It's after noon."

"Shit." I look at the clock on the microwave and she's right. I slept half the day away. I should have already done a few hours of exercise by now.

Oh well. It was worth it.

I grab a soda and sit at the kitchen table. I can feel my mom's gaze burning into me, so I look up at her. "Yes?"

She shreds the pork with two forks but keeps her eyes trained on me. "You've been out with Bree the last three nights in a row."

I nod and sip from the soda can. "Yeah."

Her lips flatten into a thin line. "You better not break that girl's heart."

"Mom, I'm your son. You should be saying *she* better not break *my* heart."

Mom rolls her eyes. "That's not happening."

I go to protest, but she cuts me off with a single look. "Honey, I love you and I've looked the other way at your partying lifestyle, and I try to stay out of your business, but this is different. She's not some random fangirl. She's a local. She lives and works at the track."

"You think I don't know this?" I say.

Mom sighs. "She's a good girl. She's smart and sweet. She's not like the other girls."

"Again," I say, unable to hide a smile when I think about Bree. "You think I don't know this? That's what makes her special."

Mom empties a jar of BBQ sauce into the crockpot. "Just don't hurt her, Zach."

"We're just friends," I say, even though I know that's a lie. I just can't stand my mom looking at me like I'm some horrible dick who treats women like shit.

"And I'm just asking you to be careful," Mom says. "Don't hurt her."

"I won't," I say just to end the conversation. But deep down I don't know if it's true. Of course I'll never purposely hurt her, but what's going to happen at the end of summer?

Guess I have all summer to figure it out.

Me: What's up?

Bree: House cleaning :(

Me: Want to hang out when you're done?

Bree: maybe…

I grin as I read her text. I wish Bree didn't work so damn much. I want to spend all of my time with her. Luckily she does work. I'm forced to spend the time she's at work focusing on working out and getting some laps in at the track. Left to my own devices, I'd curl up with Bree in my twin sized bed and never leave. It's probably a lot healthier that we spend some time apart each day.

Still, my chest aches for her while I'm waiting for her to get off work.

Tommy calls me right after my workout, asking if I want to head to Skeeter's to grab a bite. Bree will be a while, so I figure I might as well go.

I meet Tommy in the restaurant and he's already ordered a giant appetizer of cheese fries.

"Damn dude," I say, grabbing one. "Trying to make me fat?"

He chuckles. "I'm trying to make myself fat. You're supposed to have self-control."

Tommy doesn't know about my sudden infatuation with Bree, and I'd like to keep it that way. I can only imagine what he'd say, how he'd act just like my mom and tell me to stop messing around with her. As far as he knows, I've been spending all my time training and sticking to my goals.

We're almost done eating our meals when I get a phone call from Marcus, my Team Loco manager. Seeing his name on the screen makes me instantly nervous. I haven't heard from Marcus since I moved out of my old apartment. He knows I'll be training hard in the hopes that I'll qualify in the fall.

Why is he calling? This can't possibly be good.

I leave Tommy my debit card so he can pay for my meal and I slip outside to answer the call. I haven't felt this nervous in a long ass time.

"Hello?"

"My man," Marcus says. He sounds happy. I relax a little.

"What's going on?"

"You have been granted a lifeline."

I have no idea what that means. "Huh?"

"Aiden crashed last night, broke his wrist. The doctor said it won't need surgery but he's out for at least eight weeks. Bad news for him, good news for you. You can take over his spot for Team Loco this weekend."

I don't even know what to say. For a split second, I'm overcome with happiness. I mean, I feel bad for Aiden but this is like finding the golden ticket for me. A free spot on the team, no qualification necessary. I won't get the race points since I'm filling in for someone else, but I'll still be on the team and still earn money from it.

But then I picture that beautiful girl I've been spending all my time with.

"Wow," I say because it's been too long since I've said anything.

"I hope you've been training hard," Marcus says.

"Yes sir, I have."

"Great. I'll send a car to pick you up on Friday morning. Your address is still the one in Hopewell, right?"

"Yeah," I say. My throat goes dry. I don't have a choice here. I have to go.

We end the call and I stand here in the parking lot of the diner as a surreal feeling rises in my chest. It's overwhelming how terribly excited and horrified I am at the same time. I need this. I need Team Loco and I'm dying to get back on a real professional motocross track, not a small town one for amateurs.

This is my career. My life. The one thing I've worked so hard for so that I can make something of myself and give my mom the happy retirement she deserves.

I can't risk losing my spot on Team Loco, and telling Marcus no right now would be the end of me. When my team needs me, I have to be there. I signed a contract that says as much.

I have four days until I have to leave.

How the hell am I supposed to break the news to Bree?

CHAPTER 14

Bree

My mom can definitely tell something is going on with me. That's the big flaw with spending your days in close proximity while cleaning houses. She knows I'm acting differently. Happy. Yesterday, she walked in on me humming while I was cleaning a client's kitchen countertops and she gave me the weirdest look. Then it occurred to me that I never hum songs while cleaning. I flushed from head to toe and tried to act normal.

Now it's Tuesday and I had to go all day yesterday without seeing Zach. He said he had some family stuff come up and couldn't hang out yesterday, so now that I've had a whole day away from him, I feel slightly less enamored and slightly more in control of myself.

But I'm still thinking of him all day, every day. I'm like a lovestruck idiot who has been hit with Cupid's arrow and now I can't function as a normal human being anymore.

And I don't even care that I'm not quite sure what we are. For now, being with Zach means I'm not stressing about finding a real job or wondering if I should go into debt to go back to school. Right now I'm just living for the moment and it feels amazing. For once in my life, I'm not planning the next step, solidly focused on the future.

Zach makes living in the present the best type of life ever. I can't believe how different he is in real life, compared to the guy on social media. He hasn't even updated his own Instagram since he came back to Hopewell, and of course all the #ZachPena photos from other people have slowed down. Instead of fancy parties and professional motocross photos, regular people from Hopewell are tagging him in their Insta photos while they stand next to him at the local track.

In real life, Zach doesn't drink much, at least not around me. He doesn't hit up the bars or the club or anything. We went to the movies and the lake and we even went shopping for new furniture for his mom's house on Sunday. That was probably my favorite time with him. We held hands and walked the aisles of a furniture store and it all felt so real. Like a real couple. A real relationship.

But of course, that's not what we are. I'm not stupid enough to even ask that question or bring up the subject with him. That would certify me as clingy and he'd probably run the other way.

Zach probably just wants a summer fling with me. And even though deep down in my heart, I know I want more, I'm telling myself to just be cool. I'm allowed to have a summer fling, too. I just wish he wasn't so amazing. When I kissed him in the lake, I was hoping he'd just be some sexy guy to make out with. I never expected that he had an amazing personality, and a soft side, and problems of his own. Now it all feels a little too real.

Mama only has two houses to clean today since Tuesdays are always slow, and she tells me she can handle them herself and that I should take the day off. The bad news is that being off work means sitting at home with nothing to do but think about Zach. In the mornings, he works out, and around noon to four, he usually rides at the track. I've been keeping my distance while he rides because I know the practice is important to him. But sometimes, if I get home from work early enough, I'll sit near my bedroom window and watch him ride across the part of the track I can see from here.

I clean up my house a little and organize my bedroom just to pass the time. I keep an eye on my phone but I don't hear from Zach at all, which is unusual. Around four in the afternoon, I wonder if I should text him. We didn't get to hang out yesterday and now I'm dying to see him again. My whole body aches to be near him. That's how badly I've fallen for this guy.

I set my phone down and tell myself to chill out. He's not my boyfriend. He's still just some guy. So what if I make out with him on occasion? I refuse to be the girl who texts first.

The whole night goes by without a single word from him.

I can barely sleep because I'm wondering what went wrong. We spent three days together, practically attached at the hip, and everything was amazing. He told me about his life and his racing career. I told him about college and my uncertain career future.

I thought we had clicked.

So why did he ignore me all day?

On Thursday, I throw myself into my cleaning jobs with Mama. I scrub and mop and dust and organize with precision. I keep myself busy so that I don't think about *him*.

There's just no reason for a guy to be all over you and then just totally ghost you. No reason at all unless he's over me. I guess he moved on. Found another girl.

Well, good for him. I refuse to let it hurt me. I *refuse* to be hurt by Zach Pena.

Our houses are cleaned in record time due to my extra dedication to my work. Mama wants to get dinner together but I tell her I'm too tired and just want to go home. She gives me a look like she's concerned about my sudden mood change, but she doesn't say anything, which is good. I don't have any desire to lie to her and I'm certainly not going to tell her the truth.

After Dad gets off work, he and Mama go out for a dinner date. I sit on the couch in the living room and try to watch the most unromantic show I can find. I settle on a true crime series because there's nothing romantic about murder.

It's just after seven in the evening when the doorbell rings. I get up and glance out the front window before approaching the door. I see that stupid black truck parked in my driveway and my nerves all light up at once. My feelings are a mixture of anger and excitement.

I'm wearing leggings and a tank top and my hair is piled on top of my head in a messy bun, but oh well. Zach doesn't deserve to see me dressed up for him.

I pull open the door and keep my face neutral. "Yeah?" I say instead of a hello.

Zach's gorgeous face looks remorseful as hell. "Bree, I'm so sorry."

I shrug. "For what?"

"For not seeing you in two days."

Or calling, or texting, or giving me any kind of explanation, I add in my mind. Instead, I shrug again. "I don't care."

"Yeah, you do," he says softly. "I had something come up, and I really am sorry. But I'm going to make it up to you tonight."

I lift an eyebrow.

He grins. "Go pack some clothes. I got us dinner reservations and a hotel in the city."

"You did *what*?" I say, unable to hide my shock.

Zack runs a hand over his hair. "I want to make it up to you. I've missed you like crazy these last two days and I need all the time I can get with you. Please join me?"

The way he looks up at me with those puppy eyes that sparkle blue under the porch light just about melts me. Maybe he's telling the truth. Maybe his mom got sick or something and he couldn't see me because he was taking care of her.

I fold my arms over my chest, not wanting to give in too easily. "What restaurant?"

"Perry's."

I swallow. That place is expensive as hell. It's the kind of place you take a girl when you messed up bad and want to make it up to her.

"And the hotel?" I say.

"Radisson."

Nice. I can feel a smile tugging at my lips. A hotel can only mean one thing, and damn if I haven't been picturing taking him to bed, making up for that first night we had together by doing all the things I've wanted to do to him since he came back to town.

I step back and let him inside. "I'll go get packed," I say, leaving him in the living room.

I throw on a purple dress for dinner and dab some makeup on. I fix my hair so that it's in a neat bun with some curly wisps hanging down my face. Then I throw my sexiest pajamas and another outfit for tomorrow into a bag.

"Wow," Zach says when I emerge from my room. "You look hot as hell."

I don't return the compliment even though Zach looks drop dead sexy in his dark jeans that hug his thigh muscles and a blue shirt that fits him in all the right places. I'm still a little peeved, and he clearly wants to make the night special, so I'm going to let him do all the work.

We slip into our normal selves once we get to the restaurant. Zach doesn't tell me what he did over the last two days, but we talk and laugh and it all feels just like it did before he ditched me. Some of my hurt feelings fade away and I tell myself that he's probably just going through something personal and he'll tell me when he's ready. Maybe he was actually taking care of his mom because I know she has bad arthritis.

After dinner, we drive into the next big city to the Radisson. I get a little nervous with each passing minute. Soon, we'll be in a hotel room together. I've never been in a hotel room with a guy in my life.

A thrill of excitement shoots through me and then it's immediately followed by nervous energy.

At the hotel, I'm nervous as hell. We walk into the lobby and Zach gets the hotel key and then we're walking hand in hand down a plush carpeted hallway to the elevators. My heart beats like crazy as we ride up to the seventh floor. Zach stops just outside of our hotel room and he turns to me.

"Bree," he says, his voice soft as his eyes peer into mine. "I just thought we could spend time together away from our families. My childhood bedroom is—" He laughs and shakes his head. "Embarrassing, to say the least. And I missed you and wanted to hang out and since I don't have my own apartment anymore, I thought a hotel was the next best thing."

"Okay..." I say. "Why are you giving me a lecture in the hallway?"

"Sorry," he says. "I just wanted you to know that I don't...*expect*...anything."

"That's enough talking," I say. I take the hotel key from his hand and open the door. Inside, the room is luxurious in a way I've never seen before from a lifetime of staying in cheap hotels. There's one king-sized bed with satin sheets in the middle of the room. The furniture is big and fluffy and clean. It even smells nice in here, like roses and vanilla, instead of cleaning chemicals or stale musty carpet.

I drop my bag on the table next to the TV. "This place is nice."

"I like staying in the Radisson when we're on tour," Zach says, closing the door behind us and dropping his bag on the table next to mine.

"You get to stay in fancy hotels like this all the time?" I ask.

He nods. He grabs his elbow with one hand and looks around the room. "They put us up in nice places."

He looks a little distracted. Something about this confident womanizing man looking so vulnerable is an instant turn on. I feel it in my belly, the desire for him rising up into an uncontrollable need.

I walk toward him and watch his expression soften.

"Bree," he breathes as I wrap my arms around him. "There's things we should talk about."

I lean up on my toes and kiss him. "I don't want to talk."

His arms wrap tightly around me as I kiss him again. "We should though," he whispers between kissing me. "Talk, I mean."

I press against his chest and slide my hands up his neck, then pull his face down to mine. "We can talk later," I whisper into his ear. He exhales a ragged breath, and his grip on my waist tightens. I knew I'd win him over.

I grab his shirt and pull it off, tossing it over an armchair. Then I reach for his jeans and unbutton them, letting gravity assist me as I tug them down. He steps out of them, and soon he's standing before me with a raging hard on wearing only boxer briefs. He gives me a sultry grin. "Your turn."

I slip out of my dress and then take off my strapless bra. I thought I'd be more nervous, but I'm not. I'm so ready for this. So ready for him.

I step backward until I reach the bed, and then I sit on it and motion for him to join me. Zach leans over and kisses me. I let my hands tangle in his hair and I relax into the pleasure of his caressing licks and kisses. His hands roam over my body and his lips meet mine with all that passion we've kept hidden over the last few weeks.

He pulls away from the kiss and peers deep into my eyes. I grin up at him.

"Now, isn't this better than talking?"

CHAPTER 15

ZACH

Waking up with Bree in my arms is even better than I'd imagined it would be. She's so soft and angelic, curled up under the blankets next to me. I close my eyes and bury my face in her hair and enjoy the moment for as long as I can.

And then the guilt sinks in. I try to push it back, but it's overwhelming. I had a plan, and I didn't do it. I was supposed to tell her that I'm leaving, flying out to Vegas for the race next weekend. It was supposed to be the first thing I said. We could have acknowledged that this is just a fling and it's no big deal and then we could have spent one last fun night together.

But I didn't stick to the plan.

I couldn't get the words out. I didn't want the night to be darkened with the news that I'm leaving tomorrow. Bree just brings something out in me that I can't push aside. I wanted to wrap her up in my arms and never let go.

Bree opens her eyes and looks back at me. "What are you thinking about?" she asks.

"Nothing," I say.

She rolls over and gives me a look. "You're lying. I can tell you're thinking something."

I take a deep breath and sit up in bed. I can't hold off any longer. I scrub my hands over my face and then look at her.

"I got called back to Team Loco."

She sits up and gives me a curious look. "What does that mean?"

"This guy on my team got injured and can't race the rest of the summer season so I'm taking his place."

I try to say it like it's good news, because it *is* good for my career. But it's not good for us.

Bree's eyes widen and then her lips turn down. "You're leaving."

It's not a question, it's a statement.

I exhale slowly. "Yeah."

"When?"

"Tomorrow."

Her eyes flash with what can only be the feeling of betrayal. She stands up and storms across the hotel room. "How long did you know?"

I want to lie to her, but I can't. "A few days," I say, feeling fully like the asshole that I am. "I didn't know how to tell you."

"No, of course not," she snaps. "But you certainly knew how to get me into bed before you ran off." She grabs her jeans and tugs them on over her panties. She unplugs her phone and shoves it in her bag and then zips it all closed.

"Bree," I say, "It's not like that."

"No, it's exactly like that," she says, the anger in her voice cutting me like a knife. "You just wanted to get laid before you jet off and go back to your old lifestyle. You didn't change. And I'm the dumbass who thought that you did."

She walks right out the door and lets it slam closed behind her.

She has every right to be pissed at me. When I put myself in her shoes, that's what it seems like. That I used her just for sex. But that's not even close to being true. I had avoided her for the last two days because I didn't know what to do. I couldn't reconcile my feelings for her with the fact that I can't get in a relationship right now. I can't get a girlfriend. I have to focus on motocross. Even if I did let myself feel what I want to feel for Bree—what kind of relationship would we have? She'd be stuck in Hopewell missing me every weekend while I was flying around from town to town racing for Team Loco. It just doesn't work. She would have gotten hurt no matter what. So I did the right thing and I stayed away.

Until I couldn't anymore. Then I got the hotel. I was supposed to tell her the truth. I figured we'd talk about how much it sucks but then agree to stay friends.

It wasn't supposed to go like this.

I sink to the bed, my head resting in my palms.

Damn.

I'm up too early on Saturday morning. Early days usually don't bother me, but I didn't sleep at all last night. Like a fool, I'd texted Bree a few times and then called her. She didn't reply to my texts and she didn't answer her phone. Her cousin Mia had that honor.

I still remember Mia's words when she picked up my call. "She doesn't want to talk to you," she'd said. "Stop calling. My cousin is too good for you."

I drink some water and pace the small area of Team Loco's tent. We're set up in the VIP pit area of the Vegas stadium, right outside in the parking lot. In an hour or so, the pits will open up to the fans who have purchased pit passes and they'll walk around and get autographs and want to take pictures with the racers.

I'm not in the mood to meet anyone, especially the fans that I've promised to always be kind to. I don't even feel like racing today.

"What's wrong?" Clay says as he makes his way under the rope that sections off the racers from the fans. He's holding a pink cup with a thick straw in it. "You look like shit."

My other teammate Jett is right behind him, also holding a pink cup with a huge straw. "You nervous?" Jett asks. "Don't be. I know you've been gone for a few weeks, but you'll be fine once you get on the track."

I shake my head but I can't think of anything to say. I'm not nervous about the race. And maybe that's the big problem here. I don't care at all about this race. I just want to be back home with her. And she wants nothing to do with me.

"You should go to the smoothie truck down there," Clay says, pointing somewhere off to the right. "They're making free smoothies for the racers and they're delicious."

Jet nods as he drinks from his cup. "They're amazing."

I want so badly to tell them that's a good idea and then go get my own smoothie. I want things to feel like they used to when I spent all my time with these guys traveling from race to race. But my stomach is already too nervous with the ache of missing Bree and no damn smoothie is going to taste good right now.

I stop pacing and sit on one of the Team Loco branded canvas chairs. I run my hands through my hair and tell myself to get my shit together.

Jett hovers nearby, the straw of his smoothie gurgling with each sip. "Dude, what's going on?"

"Nothing," I say, trying to force a smile.

He frowns. "This doesn't seem like pre-race jitters, man. You know you're gonna do fine out there. So what's making you so stressed?"

I shake my head and exhale. "I don't know. Just not having a good day."

Jett looks like he wants to say something else, but he doesn't. He's the youngest member of Team Loco and he's our newest rookie, yet sometimes he feels older than all of us. He's just mature and confident and seems like he's never had a bad day. I don't know how he does it. But he is the son of the famous motocross racer Jace Adams, who was one of my childhood heroes. Maybe growing up in the sport with someone like that as a dad gives you a better outlook on life. When I was a kid, I had no one but my mom and the dads at the track who would help me out along the way.

I pretend like there's something on my phone worth looking at, and Jett eventually starts talking to Clay and they leave me alone.

When it's time to race, I feel the familiar tingle of adrenaline that normally comes with a race. It makes me feel a little better knowing that my body still knows what to do even if my mind is occupied. We get dressed in our race gear and the team's mechanics start our bikes and get everything ready to go.

I ride out of the parking lot in the designated pathway for racers that leads us straight into the stadium where thousands of fans wait to watch the race. We line up at the starting line and I rev my engine. It feels good to be back on my team bike, with its powerful engine and suspension that makes it far superior to my old bike at home.

Bree still floats in my mind, and I don't think I'm capable of forgetting her, not even for a twenty-minute race. The gate drops and my skill kicks in. I get a good starting position and I'm only two bikes behind Jett, who is in the lead.

I ride hard and fast and I put everything I have into this race, despite the aching pain in my chest that's throwing me off. When the checkered flag flies, I am in third place.

Not good, but not bad.

And it keeps me on the team.

I follow my teammates out of the arena and back to the pits. Some fans stand around and wave at us and I wave back, trying to put on a smile even though they can't see it through my helmet.

When we get to our tent, Marcus slaps a hand on my back and tells me I did a good job. But most of the attention is on Jett, who won the race.

I pull off my helmet and grab a bottle of water. I feel a light tap on my shoulder, and I turn around to find Keanna Park standing right in front of me. She's normally friendly and sweet but right now she looks serious.

"Let's talk."

CHAPTER 16

Bree

I haul the vacuum cleaner out of the back of Mom's car. This is the fourth house we've cleaned this morning and it's not even noon yet. I am exhausted because I haven't slept well for two days. My stupid brain won't stop thinking about that asshole who slept with me and then raced off to go be famous again.

And it doesn't help that I'm currently standing in front of his mom's house.

Since Zach is gone, I decided I can help Mama make her rounds today. Luckily my parents have no idea about my pathetic love life, and I intend to keep it that way. I'm sure Mama would want to sit down and talk about my feelings, and Dad would probably gripe at me for being stupid enough to hook up with a motocross guy. He's spent my whole life telling me that motocross guys are trouble. Who knew he was right.

I refuse to think that the ache in my chest is even close to heartache. Zach didn't break my heart. I'm not that pathetic. I refuse to be. The pain is just betrayal, I tell myself. It's the feeling of some guy being a dick. That's all.

I lug the vacuum cleaner into Ms. Pena's house and set it by the front door. I always vacuum last, so I can leave clean carpet lines behind us. Mama is cleaning the kitchen, and I know the hallway and bedrooms are my part of the job. I hold my shoulders back and stand straight and I refuse to let this hurt me. He's just some guy. I mean nothing to him, and therefore I'll make sure he means nothing to me.

I go straight into Zach's childhood bedroom and get to work. I dust and clean and tidy up. Right now it looks like a kid's room again. All traces of the grown up Zach have been packed up and taken with him. I make quick work of the job, and then I close the door and get to working on the rest of the house.

We clean three more houses until we're done for the day. My chest doesn't stop hurting. By this point, I'm more pissed off at myself than Zach. Why can't I get it together? Why can't I be like the guys who sleep around and never think twice about it? Why do I have to have all these feelings?

I actually thought I cared about Zach. I thought we had a connection.

What an idiot.

I take a long hot shower to wash off the chemicals and sweat from cleaning houses all day. Then I change into my most comfortable pajamas, a pair of soft fleece-lined leggings and a baggy T-shirt. I need to take care of myself so that my stupid wrecked heart can heal again.

I also need a job. A good job that pays well and is located anywhere else but Hopewell, Tennessee. I make a milkshake because what's better than ice cream to make you feel better, and then I sprawl out on my bed and watch TV while I open my laptop.

I am determined to find a good job. I open all the usual career websites and get to work. I apply for everything that sounds even remotely interesting, and when I'm tired of clicking through dozens of tedious job applications, I take a deep breath and send a few more.

The sooner I find a good job, the sooner I get out of here. Living on a motocross track is no way to get over the guy I was starting to fall for. I yawn and stretch out on my bed, changing positions because my elbows are getting tired.

On TV, an infomercial has started, and the two hosts are doing their best to sell me some stupid cooking appliance that looks like it'd break after one use. I check the time. It's just after eight, and I've been applying for jobs for four hours. Holy shit. If I don't get one of these jobs I'll lose my mind.

I click on the next job opening on the laptop screen in front of me. It's for a business manager position at an office park. It's one of those modern places like Google, where the building is made of glass with contemporary architecture, and hipsters abound. The job listing says you'll get free dry cleaning, free lunch in their state of the art cafeteria, and free access to their company gym that has over two hundred exercise machines. Their employee benefits are top of the line and you start out with four weeks paid vacation.

This would be an amazing job. I actually fit the requirements, too. It says they'll conduct interviews for anyone who has an associates degree or higher. They put emphasis on finding the right candidate for the job based on their personality and work ethics, not their education. Woohoo!

I open my resume and tweak it a bit so it makes me look as good as possible. Then, when I'm about to upload it, I realize I didn't even pay attention to where the job is located.

I go back and look, and my heart sinks. Nashville.

That's where Zach lives when he has his own place. Will he go back there now that he's famous again? Probably.

I grit my teeth. I can't let the fear of running into Zach stop me from applying for my dream job. I send the application.

The page refreshes and thanks me for applying. Then there's a line at the bottom of the page that makes my heart sink.

You are applicant number 4338. Due to the high number of applicants, we can't interview everyone and will therefore conduct screening and will call chosen applicants for an initial phone interview.

It goes on but I don't bother reading it all. There are over four thousand people trying to get this dream job. There's no way it'll be me.

I breathe in deeply, closing my eyes and trying to find a way to calm my nerves. I exhale, and then roll over on my bed, holding back a frustrated scream.

My phone beeps, and I reach for it, my heart pounding. Is it another message from Zach? I've been ignoring him since the day he used me and left me. But for some sick reason I still get excited when he tries to reach out to me. I know he's only doing it because he feels bad. He didn't care about me. He probably thinks I'll tell my dad and he'll get banned from Hopewell Motocross Park, so he's trying to suck up and apologize.

Yeah, well screw him.

The message isn't from Zach, though. It's an alert from Instagram. I have one new DM from Keanna Park.

Why does that name sound so familiar? I click on the message.

Hello! Is this the Bree who works at Hopewell MX Park?

I stare at her message for a long time. Sometimes people contact me out of the blue asking questions about the track. But I can't get her name out of my mind. I know I've heard it before. Her profile picture shows her as a beautiful girl about my age, with auburn hair and a pretty smile. She doesn't look familiar though, and I'm pretty sure I've never seen her around the track. I click on her profile.

Mystery solved.

She's the future Keanna Adams. As in, *Jett Adams*, as in, the swoony-hot professional motocross racer that just about every girl at the track is in love with. He comes from motocross royalty since his dad was also a famous racer back in the day. Keanna is his girlfriend, and now I know she's probably not messaging me to ask some innocent question about the track.

Because the thing is, Jett Adams is also on Team Loco.

I've already clicked on the stupid message, so she knows I've read it. I can't just ignore it because that would be weird. I reply.

Me: *Yep, that's me. Do you have a question about the track?*

Keanna: *Not exactly. I had a question about something else. Could I call you?*

I stare at the screen. How do you say hell no in a polite way?

Me: *Sorry, I'm busy at the moment. You can message me though.*
Keanna: *I'd really like to talk on the phone. It's kind of important.*

I grit my teeth. No point in dancing around the truth. If she's messaging me out of the blue it's because she's probably hanging out with Team Loco right now. Zach's messages have gone ignored so he's trying to get someone else to reach out to me.

Me: *Did Zach put you up to this?*
Keanna: *Nope. But I do want to talk about him. :) Can I please call you?*
Me: *Sorry, I'm not interested. Zach is a prick and I'm better off without him.*

My phone shows that Keanna is typing a reply. I hate myself for caring so much, but I sit up in bed and watch the screen while I wait for her next message. Minutes go by and still nothing. But it says she's typing. Either it's going to be some long diatribe begging me not to get Zach banned from the track because he used and left me, or she's not sure what to say and keeps backspacing and starting over again.

A loud banging sound makes me jump so hard I drop my phone. Someone is knocking on the door. Well, no, not *knocking*.

They're pounding as if the world is ending.

Dad is still at work and Mama is probably asleep because cleaning so many houses makes her worn out. I jump up and run to the front door. "What's going on?" Mama says sleepily. She shuffles out of her room.

"Someone's beating on the door," I say, peaking out of the peephole.

Luckily it's not some psychopath. It's just Jake, one of the other guys who works at the track. I unlock and open the door. "What's going on?"

There's a horrifying look in his eyes. He's covered in sweat and panting as if he ran over here from far away. "Call 911," he says. "Hurry!"

"Oh my God," Mama says. "What's going on?"

"Hurry!" Jake says, pushing himself into our house. "My phone is dead. I need a phone. Where's a phone?"

I run back to my room and grab my phone. There's a new message from Keanna and it is pretty long, but there's no time for that now. I go to the call screen and type 911 and then hand it over.

"It's your dad," Jake tells me as he presses the phone to his ear. "It's bad."

CHAPTER 17

ZACH

I wake up in an unfamiliar place. It smells delicious though, like pancakes and coffee and syrup. I stretch out my limbs and yawn, and then quickly remember where I am. Jett's house.

We have five days off until the next Team Loco race and I had nowhere to go. I don't have an apartment anymore, and after my mom found out that I'd accepted my job back on Team Loco without telling Bree, she was pissed. She'd told me that Bree deserved an explanation. I know she's right. God, I know she's right. But I don't want to go home because of how shitty I feel now. My mom will only make me feel worse. And being home will remind me that Bree isn't talking to me. There's no place in Hopewell for me now.

Even Keanna and her magical thinking weren't enough to make Bree talk to me again. After the races last night, Keanna had pulled me aside and asked how things were going. I guess she noticed that my social media accounts weren't as busy as they used to be and she thought something was wrong. She was right. I spilled my guts like an idiot and told her everything. Then she got all excited and said we could totally fix the problem with Bree. She said all she'd have to do is talk to her. She'd explain things in the language that girls use to talk to each other and it'd all be fine. Keanna was pretty damn confident about it all.

And yet, here we are a day later and Bree still hasn't messaged me. So Keanna was wrong.

She doesn't get it. She met Jett when she was a teenager and they fell in love and stayed in love. Jett never screwed her over the way I screwed over Bree so she just doesn't get it. She'll never understand. Her life is this perfect fairy tale. She even lives next door to

Jett, although I know they're getting their own place soon. I've seen Jett looking up floor plans online and talking to the same contractor that built his parent's house. He's planning on buying the land next to them and building Keanna's dream home for her.

"You awake?" Jett says. He crawls out of his bed and runs his hands through his hair.

I'm sleeping on the futon in his room. I sit up. "Yeah. You think there's enough food for us?" I ask, motioning to the door where the smells of breakfast are wafting up here.

"Of course," Jett says, pulling on a shirt. "My mom makes a ton of food."

Mrs. Adams is pretty hot for a mom. She's also younger than most of my friend's moms. I avert my gaze though, because I'm not going to be the pervert who checks out my friend's mom. I know that pisses him off. It would piss me off too if I were in his situation.

Mrs. Adams has made a ton of food, just like Jett said she would. I join their happy family at the big dining table. Jace Adams was one of my idols when I was a kid, and it's cool as shit to be in his home now. He has his little girl Brooke sitting in his lap since she doesn't want to sit in her high chair. He feeds her bites of his food. It's kind of cute and makes me think about kids for the first time. It's never even crossed my mind if I wanted to have kids of my own. I guess I never thought about it.

Jett's whole family is something to be admired. They care about each other and they get along well and they've got each other's backs. They own a motocross track which is right next door. I can't imagine how badass that would be. I never pictured myself having kids, but I can definitely picture myself running my own track. I know the owner of Hopewell Motocross Park is getting old, and maybe he'll retire someday. Maybe he'll want to sell the track.

I eat my French toast and let my imagination run away with me. I picture buying the track from him and then marrying Bree and we could live there together running our own track just like Jace does with his wife. We could have kids. We could raise them in motocross. Maybe I'd have a kid who goes on to live out my legacy.

Jett's mom bursts out into laughter, taking me out of my daydream. I look over and see that she's laughing at her daughter, who has decided to dunk her chubby toddler fingers into the syrup and then press it to her dad's face.

"You're lucky you're so cute," Jace tells her, kissing the top of her head. He stabs his fork into scrambled eggs and takes a bite.

"You want me to hold her while you wash that off?" Mrs. Adams says.

"Nah," he says, shaking his head. I'm sure there will be more where that came from."

Brooke giggles and claps her hands in delight. She's a really cute kid. I bet Bree would love her.

Jett leans over to me. "Sorry," he says. "My parents have gotten very lame since the baby was born."

"I heard that!" Mrs. Adams says. She throws a plastic toddler fork at him. "We are not lame. We're cool as hell."

"Damn straight," Jace says.

I laugh. Yeah, they're not exactly cool anymore, but they have something that most people would envy. A loving relationship, a badass house, and a great family.

I know I don't deserve any of that but it doesn't stop me from daydreaming. I think the best way to settle down would be to do it with a motocross girl and to stay in the motocross world. There's no better place to live.

Again, I think about Hopewell and wonder if old man Grant has any plans for it after he gets too old to keep running the place. I don't think he has any kids, so I doubt anyone is going to inherit it. Maybe he'll sell it to me.

"You wanna go ride?" Jett asks when we're finished with breakfast.

"Hell yeah."

We don't have our Team Loco bikes since those stay with the team, but Jett has several personal bikes and they're all professional grade. We suit up and take a couple for a ride.

The motocross park that Jett's dad owns is called The Track. It's a fitting name, but it's also kind of funny. It's like they couldn't think of anything else to call it so they just called it what it is.

All of my frustrations with life seem to disappear when I'm riding. Racing may be my passion, but there's something great about just riding on an open track without the pressure of the checkered flag or the stress of having an audience.

We ride for an hour, never getting off the track. Jett chases me and then I chase him and we push each other to go faster and hone our skills. But it's not as aggressive as during a real race because we don't want to do something stupid and get injured.

I pull over to get some water and that's when I notice the girl sitting on the bleachers. She's the only spectator out here. She waves at me and I ride my bike over there, then pull off my helmet.

On the track, Jett flies by and does a no-handed jump to show off for his girlfriend.

"Any news?" I ask her.

Keanna frowns. "No. I sent her this long message last night and I thought for sure that it would change her mind. It says she read it but she never replied."

My heart tightens but I shrug my shoulders like it's no big deal. "Told you it wouldn't work. Life isn't some happy love fairy tale."

Keanna gives me a look. "I never said it was, Zach. Life can be really hard."

There's something in her eyes that tells me she's dealt with a life that was hard. Now I feel bad for what I said.

"Sorry. I know you're just trying to help."

"She might just need time to think about it," Keanna says. "I'll let you know if she writes back to me."

"Thanks."

The rumble of an approaching dirt bike signals that Jett finally got off the track. He parks his bike next to mine and hops off, leaving his helmet on the bike's handlebars. "Hey beautiful," he says, jogging up the bleachers to where his girlfriend sits. He leans over and kisses her. She smiles up at him.

Ugh.

The last thing I want to see right now is a happy couple in love. No freaking thanks. I crank up my bike and get back on the track. But feeling the power of the bike beneath me doesn't do much to erase the thoughts that are swirling around in my head. I shouldn't have let Keanna talk to Bree. The only person who should talk to her is me. I screwed this up and I have to make it right. If there's still a chance for making things right.

After lunch, Jett and I hit up the gym. They also have a gym on site at The Track. It's a state of the art facility too, and I'm once again jealous of Jett's badass life.

We blast the music and hit the weights and I pour all of this pain into working out. I try not to think about Bree, but she's the only thing on my mind. I hurt her. I hurt myself. I should have never taken her to that hotel. I should have been honest with her. Hell, I should have listened to Tommy and stayed far away in the first place. This summer was not about finding my dream girl. It was supposed to be about motocross and I went and screwed it all up.

I stare at my phone and I want to text her so bad. I want to call her. I want to hop on a plane and fly to Tennessee and confess my love for her.

Whoa. Did I just think the word *love*? I am in way over my head.

I set my phone down and lay back on the weight bench. I'll never get over her if I keep thinking about calling her.

"Hey, Zach?" Keanna says over the loud music. I don't even know when she got here but now she's walking toward me.

I sit up. She looks concerned and her phone is in her hand and now all I'm thinking about is Bree. Maybe Bree wrote her back. Maybe it's bad news.

She turns down the music and walks over to me. Jett looks over from where he's lifting weights. "Everything okay?" he says.

"I don't know," Keanna says. "Something happened at Hopewell."

I lift an eyebrow. "Bree?"

"No," Keanna says, shaking her head. "It's not about her. She hasn't replied to me yet, but I just saw on the Hopewell Motocross page... There's been some kind of accident." She turns her phone toward me. "Did you know him?"

All the air rushes out of my lungs as I stare at the Facebook post on the Hopewell Motocross Page.

Hopewell will be closed today. Our groundskeeper Josh Grayson has been critically injured. Please keep him and his family in your prayers.

CHAPTER 18

Bree

The smell of this hospital makes me want to throw up. There's something about all the sterile, stark white, medical crap that I just hate. I hate it all. I can't stand being here surrounded by the sounds of the machines that are keeping my dad alive.

I hate that my dad is here.

He was working on the tractor when the jack that had it hoisted up in the air cracked and broke. Dad heard the sound fast enough to try to get out, but he wasn't fast enough. The tractor fell and crushed his lower half. I've been told by every doctor here that if my dad had been any slower, the tractor would have killed him. Crushed his head or his chest instead of his legs. You can live without legs. You can't live without a chest.

I'm having a hard time seeing the "good" in how things turned out. My dad is critically injured. When he got here they rushed him into surgery where he got pins and screws put in his pelvis. His leg bones have been pieced back together and they're monitoring for internal bleeding. So far, so good. But my dad is old. Older people have a harder time getting better.

Because of the immense amount of pain, they have him sedated. It's hard to look at him lying there all ashen in the hospital bed and not feel like he might be dead. The steady rise and fall of his chest is the only thing that lets me know he's still in there, still fighting.

Last night the doctors pulled Mama and me aside and told us that if Dad's bones healed properly that he could be walking as soon as one year from now. The doctor said it like it was a good thing. Like twelve months of being off work is going to be just fine and dandy for this family. Yeah, well, it's not.

Not to mention the fact that Mama and I will need to take care of him once he gets to come home. Don't get me wrong, I would do anything for my dad, but that means we'll have less time to work if we're caring for my dad. Less work means less money.

I stand up from the cold plastic hospital chair and begin pacing the room again. I keep trying to sit still and just be here for my dad, but I can't. I'm so stressed over the future and worried for my dad that I just can't think straight.

Mama walks back into the hospital room carrying two hot coffees. She hasn't slept or showered in the two days since this happened and she looks like it. Dark circles ring her eyes as she hands me one of the coffees. "You should sit down, hija," she says softly. "You're going to pace a hole in the floor."

I take a sip of coffee and glance back at my sleeping dad. Mama puts a hand on my shoulder. "Bree, take a breath. It'll be okay."

We've been doing this, going back and forth on who is freaking out. The first twenty-four hours I was pretty much in shock but Mama was crying and freaking out. I comforted her and told her it'd be okay. I took her down to the hospital's gift shop as a distraction when Dad was in surgery. Then she felt better when he got out and the doctors told us he should be able to walk again someday.

That's when I freaked out and she comforted me. But Mama doesn't realize that my freak outs are different from hers. Yeah, I'm worried about Dad and I hate that he's going through this, but I can't stop thinking about the future. Money. Bills.

Our mobile home is free because Dad is the groundskeeper of the track. Even though we've lived there all my life, it's still not our house. We never made payments on it. The house is a perk for dad's job. Now that he won't be able to do the job, are we going to get evicted?

I briefly consider trying to do his job myself but I don't know anything about driving tractors or heavy machinery or constructing a new dirt bike track from blueprints. It's all way over my head.

I finish my coffee and tell Mama that I have to pee, but really I walk down the hallway to the waiting room and I plunk down in the uncomfortable chairs and start looking up apartments. Even though Hopewell is a small town, there's not much Mama and I could afford on our incomes. I really need a job. A real, salary-paying job. And then I could work the track on the weekends and help Mama clean houses. She can stay home with Dad during the day and clean houses in the evenings. We'll have to find a way to make it work.

A knot digs into my stomach because it's not as easy as saying I'll "just get a job". I've been applying for jobs forever and no one ever calls me back. Not to mention, there are no good jobs in Hopewell. I've been applying in all the big cities because I want to move away and start my life over.

Once again, I feel the pang of loss as I think about Zach. Everything has been so crazy lately that I've barely had time to let my heart hurt over him. But just thinking about moving away reminds me of what I was running away from.

I want to take a stack of magazines off this waiting room table and smack myself in the face with them. I don't, because God knows what germs are on them, but ugh. I am not allowed to even think about Zach right now. Screw him. I never even read that long message Keanna sent me because I've been too busy with my dad. I don't think I'll read it at all. There's just no point.

Right now I need to figure out a way to make enough money for when we're kicked out of the house we don't own.

I look up apartments online and save a few that seem mildly affordable. There's a knock on the wall and I look up to see a familiar face.

"There you are," Grant Perkins says. He's the owner of the track. My dad's boss. He smiles at me but all it does is make me nervous. I was just thinking about him and how he'll probably kick us out of our house until my dad can work again.

"Can you join me?" he asks. I'm not sure where he wants us to go, but I get up and follow him back to my dad's hospital room.

Inside, he hugs my mom and tells her that he's confident my dad will be okay. Then he turns to both of us. My heart pounds. Grant has always been a nice guy and he's like a part of the family, but is he seriously about to talk to us about our living situation?

"I know you're in for a long recovery," he says solemnly. "I just want you to know that I'll be here to help in any way I can."

"Thank you," Mama says. She looks at me and squeezes my hand.

Grant reaches into his pocket and pulls out an envelope. He holds it out to my mom. "I want you to have this."

I watch her open it. It's some kind of official document. Tears flood into her eyes and she puts a hand over her mouth. "We can't accept this!" she says.

Grant shakes his head. "Yes, you can. I should have done it a long time ago."

Mom hands me the paper while she hugs him and I read over it. It's the deed to our house. He's giving us the house.

He's giving us the house! Holy crap!

"Thank you," I say, rushing forward to hug him myself.

Grant chuckles. "You're both quite welcome. I want you to know that you always have a place at Hopewell. Even if Josh can't get back to work for years. Or ever. This place is home to you all and I want you there. You're like my family."

Mama is full on crying now. "This means so much," she says. I can see the relief in her eyes and I realize she was probably just as worried as I was.

"Hopewell Motocross park wouldn't be the same without you," Grant says. "You let me know if you need anything, you hear? Right now I've got the guys building a wheelchair ramp on your porch. It'll be ready when Josh gets released."

I can't help myself as I throw my arms around the old man for another hug. I don't know why I worried that he might kick us out if Dad can't work anymore. He's a good guy. He's been around for as long as I can remember. Hopewell Motocross Park has been around for as long as I can remember. This little town is my life. The people are my friends. The motocross track means everything to me. I can't believe I ever wanted to move away to a big city. No big city could ever mean this much to me. No one gives you free houses in a corporate job. *This* is the place for me. I can't believe it took me so long to realize it.

I want to stay in Hopewell with the people who are my family and the people who are like family. Finding a job might be tough, but I want to make my life here, just like my parents did all those years ago.

"Thank you," I tell Grant. "You have no idea how much this means to us."

CHAPTER 19

ZACH

I read all of the Facebook comments. Most people don't know the details, but it sounds bad. Really bad.

Jett and Keanna are watching me while I dig through all the information I can find online. We've put the bikes back up and now we're all sitting on Jett's huge back patio near the pool.

"I have to go to Hopewell," I say, setting my phone down. "I need to check on Mr. Grayson."

"Did you know him pretty well?" Jett asks. He doesn't know about my Bree drama—at least I don't think he does. Keanna might have told him but he hasn't said anything. I feel like I can trust Keanna to keep my embarrassing secrets, but she and Jett also have this seriously close relationship where I bet they tell each other everything.

"Yeah," I say, feeling my chest constrict. "I've known him ever since I started riding. He's worked at the track forever. He's a great guy." I take a deep breath and let it out in a huff. "He could be dying for all I know, because no one is posting any damn details. Thoughts and prayers aren't helping me figure out what's going on."

"Maybe you could call someone?" Keanna says.

"Maybe," I say, knowing full well that I could call up Grant Perkins and ask him for information. But Mr. Grayson is more than just the guy who works at the track. He's Bree's dad. I need to be there for her.

I stand up. "I need a ride to the airport."

"Marcus wants us in Cali tomorrow," Jett says. "Think you can do both?"

"Tomorrow?" I say, glancing at my phone to check the date. "The race is three days away."

Jett shrugs. "He wants us early for practice. He sent an email."

I check my email, and sure enough there's a message from our manager. Dammit. "I don't care," I say, shoving my phone in my pocket. "I'm gonna go pack up my stuff and then I'll take the first flight to Tennessee.

Jett and Keanna share a look but I don't care what they think of me. I head inside to pack my things. Marcus will be pissed if I'm not there tomorrow, especially since I'm finally back on the team. With a sigh, I know I need to tell him. I can't just *not* show up.

I sit on Jett's futon and call my manager. He answers in a cheerful tone. Well, that's about to change.

"Hey, Marcus," I say, feeling a flutter of nerves in my stomach. What the hell am I doing? I just got back on the team. "I have some bad news. I need to fly back home for a couple days, but I'll be in Cali for the race this weekend."

"What's going on?" Marcus asks, sounding more concerned than pissed off. "Is your mom okay?"

I'm tempted to lie and say she's sick, but I don't want that kind of bad karma to come back to me.

"Yeah, she's fine, but it's another—uh—emergency. A very close family friend is in ICU and I need to visit him. And his family."

Marcus sighs and I can feel his frustration coming through the line. "You'll be back to race this weekend."

It's not a question. "Yes, sir."

Jett drives me to the airport but Keanna stays behind to babysit her brother and Jett's sister while their parents go out for lunch. I find a flight on my phone and book the next one. Unfortunately, it's two hours from now, so I wander around the Houston airport looking at the various shops and places to eat. I can't eat anything because my stomach is too twisted up. I feel so bad for Mr. Grayson. Critical condition means he could be close to death. What the hell happened to him? I bet Bree is freaking out. She's very close with her parents.

I stare at my phone and consider sending her a message. Just something casual like, "I heard about your dad and I hope he's doing okay." Or "Thinking about you and your dad." Ugh, no those are both awful. I can't express my concerns for her over a text message. I need to see her in person.

When my plane lands, I catch an Uber back home because my mom is still at work, but when my Uber pulls up to my house, Mom is just getting home.

She looks concerned when a strange car pulls up in the driveway, but then her expression turns to confusion when she sees me get out. "Zach?" she says. Then she sighs. "Did you get kicked off the team again?"

"Mom, no." I help her carry in groceries from the trunk. "I'm here to check on Mr. Grayson."

"Grayson?" she says, unlocking the front door. "The guy who works at the track?"

"Yeah," I say. "Do you know what happened to him?"

"I don't even know what you're talking about," Mom says. "Is he okay?"

I shrug. "Online it says he's in critical condition at the hospital."

"Holy shit," Mom says. "Wow, I haven't heard a word. Of course, I don't get online much and I'm not up to date with the motocross world anymore."

I grab a snack from the pantry because now I'm pretty hungry from skipping lunch. "I'm just here to visit him real quick and then I have to head to California for the race this weekend."

"Well it's nice to see you," Mom says, squeezing me into a hug.

I take a shower and try to relax as much as possible before I head to the hospital. I can't stand the thought of Bree kicking me out the second she sees me. She might do it, too. But I want to be there for her and her dad. Mr. Grayson was like family to me back when I lived here and rode at the track every day. I really hope he's going to be okay.

At the hospital, I stop in the gift shop and get some flowers. Then I finally find someone who works here and is helpful enough to tell me that Mr. Grayson is on the third floor in ICU. I make my way up there only to get stopped by the stern-faced nurse at the nurse's station. She holds out her hand for the flowers. "What room are these for?"'

"Whichever room Mr. Grayson is in," I say, handing them over. "Can I go see him?"

"Are you family?"

I bite my lip. "Not exactly, but we're like family."

"Real family only," she says without a hint of sympathy. "You can wait in the waiting room to talk to family members if you want."

I put my hands on the counter. "Can I please just go back there and look inside?" I ask. "I want to see him."

"Sorry. Family only until he's out of ICU."

Another nurse walks up wearing purple scrubs that have Scooby Doo all over them. She's younger, with long blonde hair pulled in a low ponytail and three silver earrings in each ear. "Oh my God," she says, looking at me with that look I get a lot. "You're Zach Pena, right?"

I want to roll my eyes. Now is not the time for a gushing fan, but then I realize that maybe a gushing fan *is* what I need right now.

"That's me," I say, flashing her a smile that I know will make her swoon.

Her whole face lights up. "I'm a huge fan! My cousins race motocross and I used to watch you race back in the day. Now I watch you on TV, how cool is that?"

"That's why I'm here," I say, using my flirty voice. "My friend Mr. Grayson is in here and he works at the local track. I just really want to see him before I head off to Cali for the race this weekend."

Her smile turns a little sad. "I wish I could let you back," she says, biting her bottom lip.

That first nurse I talked to has walked away, but this nurse glances around and then looks back at me. "I really can't, though. I'd get in trouble."

"I understand," I say, sighing. "I just want to know if he's okay."

"I can't really say anything either but..." She glances around to make sure we're alone. "They think he will recover," she whispers.

"What happened?" I whisper back.

"Tractor fell on him." Her voice is so soft I have to halfway listen and halfway read her lips.

My eyes widen. "Holy shit," I say at normal volume.

She nods. "His family members are in there right now and they'll probably come out soon. They come and go a lot, so you can just wait until they do."

"Thanks," I say, drumming my fingers on the countertop. I'm not sure what Bree will do when she sees me, but I hope she'll understand that I'm here because I care.

I make my way down the hallway to the waiting room. It's cold in here and smells like cleaning chemicals. The chairs are all hard plastic, which sucks. There's a TV on the wall that's playing some God-awful daytime talk show. I sit in the corner and try to get comfortable by stretching across two chairs. I really hope the wait isn't long.

Maybe as soon as that first nurse delivers my flowers to Mr. Grayson's room, Bree will come out here to thank me in person. I wrote a little note on the card in the flowers and signed it with my name. Or maybe she'll see they're from me, throw them in the trash and have security escort me out.

I take a deep breath and hope for the best. My eyes get heavy and I realize I barely slept last night. Then I rode Jett's dirt bike for hours and then hopped on a flight and barely had any food all day. I'm exhausted.

My eyes flutter closed and I rest my head against the wall behind me. It is not comfortable. There's no way I'll fall asleep like this. But somehow, I do.

I don't know how much time has passed when I become aware of my surroundings. The room is cold, and the smell is annoying. My eyes are still closed and there's a cramp in my neck. I yawn and my eyes flutter open. There's a shadow hovering over me. No, not a shadow.

A girl.

Bree Grayson is standing right in front of me.

CHAPTER 20

Bree

This is the last person I expected to find when the nurse said someone was waiting for me. I expected extended family members, or one of Dad's coworkers from the track. But the gorgeous, impossibly good-looking guy slouched across two chairs in the waiting room was not on my mind.

His eyes open and he blinks quickly, adjusting to the harsh lights of this little waiting room. He sits up and runs his hands over his hair. "Hi."

I fold my arms across my chest. "What are you doing here?"

"I came as soon as I found out. How are you? Are you okay? Is your dad okay?"

I can see the mountain of emotions behind his eyes and I know he's at least being honest about his worry for my dad. But I don't uncross my arms. I want to know why he's here. *Why.* Because everyone else who knows my dad from the track has sent their well wishes online or in cards. They haven't dropped everything and flown to another state.

I stare at him until his gaze falls to the floor. "Bree…"

"Why are you here?" I say again.

"I told you," he says, standing up. I take a step backward. It's hard to be intimidating when he's now towering over me. He reaches out and brushes his fingers across my arm. "I'm here to see if you're okay."

I grit my teeth. I can feel my heart loosening up even though I want to keep hating him. "Dad is…" I pause, looking at the floor. I don't even know what to say. I take a deep breath. "He'll survive. Most likely. I mean unless there's any crazy complications or something, but he should be okay. He got out of surgery just fine."

Zach's brows pull together. "That's good news. Can I ask what exactly happened to him? The post on the Hopewell Facebook page was pretty vague."

I can't stand telling the story because every time I do, I visualize the scene in my mind. It's horrifying. It's been haunting my nightmares and I didn't even witness it firsthand. Maybe my imagination is worse than real life.

I take a seat because otherwise I might throw up. Zach sits next to me, his knees angled toward mine. He puts a hand on my shoulder. I want to shrug him off and tell him to go to hell, but I don't. I concentrate instead on telling him what happened.

"My dad was working on the tractor. That big one they use to till up the dirt on the track?"

He nods. I swallow. "It was up in the air on a jack and the jack broke and the tractor fell down. Dad managed to crawl out as fast as he could, but his legs got crushed. There were other guys around and they tried lifting it off of him but it was really heavy. They said the paramedics arrived with the jaws of life in just enough time to save my dad."

Tears flood my eyes. I stare at the white tiled floor and try to concentrate on not getting sick to my stomach. Dad is all bandaged and casted but I don't even want to imagine what his legs look like underneath it all. Or the unimaginable pain he was in before the ambulance got to him and gave him medication.

"Holy shit," Zach breathes. "Wow. Oh my God."

He rests his head in his hands for a second and then looks up at me. "I'm so glad he's alive."

"Me too," I say. Hot tears are on the verge of spilling out of my tired eyes. I've cried so much lately and I'm sick of it.

"Why did you come here? You could have just called and gotten the information."

He looks me dead in the eyes. "Would you have answered?"

I swallow. "Probably not."

"So I had to come," he says all matter of factly.

I heave a sigh. "What about your career? What about Team Loco?"

He shakes his head. "It doesn't matter."

"Really?" I say sarcastically. "It's the reason you left me in the first place."

"Okay," he says, exhaling. He really does look like he feels like shit, which makes me a little happy. "It does matter. But only because it's my career. It's the only thing I'm good at and it's how I earn money to make a life for myself." His eyes drift up to mine. "To make a life for *us*. If you'd have me."

The lump in my throat grows so big it might suffocate me. What the in the world am I supposed to say to that?

Zach holds my gaze, like he's eager to know my response to his unasked question. He would be earning a living for us if I wanted him to. Do I want him to?

The sound of footsteps makes me look back toward the hallway. I'm saved from having to answer because my mom walks in looking thin and frail but surprisingly upbeat.

"Honey," she says, giving me a smile that kind of looks like a frown. Her eyes flit to Zach. She smiles politely at him. "Hello."

"Hi Mrs. Grayson," Zach says, standing up to greet her. "I'm Zach Pena. I've known your husband my whole life and I just wanted to come see if I could be of any help."

Mama pulls him into a hug. She's lucky. She doesn't know him like I know him. I wonder if she'd be hugging him if she knew he slept with me and then got on a plane the next day?

"There is a way you can help," she says, which surprises me. What could he possibly do?

She looks at me. "Do you have a car? Can you take Bree home?"

"Yes, of course," Zach says, sounding eager to help.

"I'm not going home!" I say, bolting up from my chair.

"Honey, you've been here for two days straight. You need a shower and a change of clothes." Mama puts a hand on my shoulder. "It'll be good for you."

I grit my teeth. "I don't want to go."

"It'll be good for you," she says again, unrelenting. "Just get a shower and some food and come right back."

"I'll take her to Skeeter's," Zach says. "I can bring you back some food too, if you'd like."

"That would be wonderful," Mama says. "Thank you."

And then she gives me a quick hug and shoos me out of the room with Zach, trusting him to take care of me. Ha. If she only knew.

I walk silently down to the elevator next to Zach. Although a shower sounds good and food that didn't come from the hospital cafeteria *really* sounds good, I don't want to admit that Mama was right. She hasn't left the hospital, so why should I?

I'm silent on the whole drive back to my house. Part of it is just so I can punish Zach and make him feel awkward. The other part of me just doesn't have any energy to say anything to the guy who broke my heart. I'd had so many strong feelings for him and then he just left.

We roll to a stop at an intersection that's close to my house. I look over at him and he's looking at me. He gives me the softest smile. I turn away.

At my house, Zach cuts the engine and follows me up to the front door. I know he has to stay here because he has to drive me back to the hospital but I hate that we're standing here on the porch together. It reminds me so much of the last time he was here, when I boldly pulled him into my room and—yeah, I can't think of that.

The air smells like freshly cut lumber. Grant wasn't kidding about the wheelchair ramp. It's already finished and it looks pretty good. I unlock the front door and go inside, then turn straight for my bedroom. I figure Zach can fend for himself in my tiny living room.

Taking a shower does feel amazing. I stand under the warm water and let it wash away the anguish. Worries over my dad, and money, and what our life will be like once he comes home. The pain of losing Zach and then seeing him show up like everything will be okay. How can it be okay when he's just going to leave again? I can't date a guy who is well known for hooking up with hot girls in every city he goes to. That would be almost as stupid as having a one night stand in a hotel room with him.

I turn the shower hotter to wash away my feelings. I soap up and shampoo my hair and feel it relax my shoulders a little bit. Finally, when the water runs cold, I have to get out and face reality again.

I throw on a clean outfit that's comfortable enough for sitting in a hospital all day, and grab my phone charger. I've been using the one Mama keeps in her purse but we really need two of them. I brush my wet hair and twist it up in a bun.

When I leave my room, Zach is sitting on the couch. "You look beautiful," he says.

The way he says it with that deep sexy voice of his stirs up something in my belly. I want to launch myself at him, throw my arms around his neck and straddle him to the couch and have my way with him.

Luckily, I'm smarter than that. "What did you mean in the hospital?" I ask, glaring at him. "When you were talking about money?"

He knows exactly what I'm talking about. "Team Loco is my career. It'll only last a few years and then I'll be set for life. I could take care of us."

"Us," I say.

He nods. "Bree ... I'm crazy about you."

"You're a womanizer," I say, keeping my composure cold and uncaring. "You hook up with girls you don't even know. You use them and you leave them."

He flinches. "That was the old me."

I snort. "Right. Of course."

"Bree, you have to believe me." He gets up from the couch and walks over to me, putting a hand on my waist. "It's not like that anymore. You are the girl I want. The only one I want."

I can feel my heart cracking apart. All those protective walls I built around it are about to be breached. I inhale deeply and stare at his chest because I can't look into his eyes right now.

"I don't believe you," I whisper.

"Bree..." He sounds like he's in pain. Good. He caused me a hell of a lot of pain. "Please."

Before I know what's happening, his fingers are under my chin, tilting my face up to meet his. He smells amazing. His other hand slides around my waist, tugging me a little closer to his rock hard chest.

I put one hand on his shoulder to steady myself and I can feel his heartbeat. It's racing, just like mine. His lips drop down to mine, and for a very small moment, I am leaning up to kiss him back, and everything feels perfect.

Then I come to my senses.

I step backward, feeling physical pain when his body is no longer pressed against mine. I shake my head and press my lips together in a flat line. "No," I say. "You can't do this. I'm not just some girl you can sleep with when you're in town."

"I never said you were," Zach says, his expression pained. "Bree, you're so much more than that."

I shake my head. I won't let his words get to me. I won't be the foolish idiot to falls for a guy who will only fly away and go hook up with whatever girl he meets next.

"Why are you stringing me along like this? I'm not stupid, Zach."

"Bree, I'm not—" he says, but I shake my head again and point to the door.

"Just go."

"I need to drive you back," he says.

"I have a car," I snap. "I'll drive myself back."

"I don't have to leave for a few more days," Zach says, running an anxious hand through his hair. "Please. Just let me stay with you. I'll do whatever I can to convince you that I'm serious. I want to be with you, Bree. No one else."

"And yet you're still going to leave," I say, refusing to be swayed by a sexy man and his well-rehearsed lies. "So just cut to the chase and do it now."

CHAPTER 21

ZACH

If this were the movies, things would be different. As I stand here on her front porch while she's kicking me out, the movie version would make the sky would crackle with thunder and then rain would start pouring all over me. She'd see me standing here, looking sad and heartbroken in the rain and she'd run after me, deciding that she loves me. We'd kiss and hold each other as the romantic storm gets us soaking wet. We'd laugh about it. We'd have a happily ever after.

But this isn't a movie.

The hot summer sun blazes down on me, threatening to make me sweaty if I stand here too long. I give Bree one last look, hoping she'll change her mind, but she doesn't. Her arms are crossed, her lips are pressed into a flat line, and she's got one hand on the front door eagerly waiting to close it behind me.

"Call me if you change your mind," I say, knowing it's probably useless. I turn around and step off the porch, hearing the door close behind me. It smacks closed with a finality that makes the hairs on the back of my neck stand up.

This can't be the end of us.

I hope she just needs some time. She's dealing with a lot right now and maybe once her dad gets better she'll consider giving me another chance.

The worst part of all of this is that she's not wrong. Not in the slightest. I was a prick. I did hook up with girls I didn't even know. I lived the life of a player.

I guess I never thought I'd find someone I wanted to settle down with. I never thought of the consequences because I never imagined I'd meet a girl like Bree. And now all those months of being a dumbass are catching up with me.

I try to imagine a life where Bree was the one hooking up with guys instead of the other way around. It makes my blood boil. I hate the thought of another man touching her. Kissing her lips. Making her happy. Giving her everything I want to give her.

I want it to be me. I know I don't deserve her, but I want her to be mine.

I haven't even considered booking a flight to Cali since I thought I would be here a few days. I drive back to my mom's house feeling defeated and rejected and pissed off at my former self. This trip did not go the way I'd hoped it would.

Mom is watching TV when I get home. Her face falls when she sees me. "Is it bad?"

"Is what bad?" I say, because she can't possibly be talking about my love life and that's the only thing I'm thinking right now.

"Mr. Grayson."

"Oh." I run a hand through my hair and sit next to her on the couch. "Yeah. He will survive, but it's bad."

Mom listens carefully while I tell her everything that Bree told me about her dad. Mom's face scrunches up in pain when I describe his injury. "Holy shit," she says, putting a hand to her mouth. "That's horrible."

"Yeah."

"I'm going to cook for them," she says, sitting up. "His poor wife and daughter must be miserable. I'll make them a basket of homemade foods for the hospital and I can call the other motocross moms in town and see about arranging a schedule. We can bring them meals every day for the next few months. That way they don't have to worry about it."

I smile. "You are the best, Mom."

"Aw, son," she says, playfully slapping my arm. "It's what the motocross family does. When you were a kid, I got so much help from the motocross parents. Mr. Grayson was always so great to us. I'm happy to help out."

I lean over and wrap my mom in a hug. She's so much shorter than I am and it's kind of funny since I'm the kid and she's the parent. But I swallow her up with my hug and bury my face into her hair and take a deep breath. I love my mom. She's always taken such good care of me and never cared about herself. It reminds me why I pursued professional motocross in the first place. My mom is my rock. I want to give her a better life. I do all of this for her.

When I release her from my bear hug, her expression grows concerned. "What's going on?" she asks. "I know it's sad about Mr. Grayson but you seem like something else is bothering you."

I chew on the inside of my lip. I've never really talked about girls with my mom, mostly because I've never had a specific girl to talk about. And she did warn me not to break Bree's heart and that's exactly what I did.

I shake my head and stare up at the ceiling. "It's Bree."

Mom watches me, her expression is half concerned and half *told-you-so*. "What happened?" she asks.

I heave a sigh. I will not tell her the details about that night at the hotel, that's for damn sure, but maybe I can tell her some of it.

"Well ... I like her, Mom. A lot."

She smiles softly, like she's seeing me in a different light. I shake my head. "No, that's a bad thing. I mean, she liked me too but then I got asked to go back to Team Loco. I thought we'd have the summer together, you know? I had given up on Team Loco for the summer and I thought I'd find a way to date her and somehow make it work in the fall but... it all happened too fast and now I'm back on the team and she wants nothing to do with me."

"Nothing at all?" Mom asks. "She doesn't want to do a long distance thing?"

I swallow. Well, the truth is a little more than that, but I nod. "I guess she thinks I can't be trusted to be faithful if I'm on the road."

"Ah," Mom says with a knowing nod. "Do you really like her?"

"Yes."

"I mean *really* like her. Would you be loyal to her if you were in a relationship and you were on the road?"

"Of course," I say, feeling a little offended that she'd even ask that. "I would never cheat on her."

Mom nods, like this was the right thing to say. "So all you have to do is prove it to her."

"She doesn't want anything to do with me."

"Maybe not now, but you can change her mind."

"How?" I ask. "I've already begged and pleaded with her."

Mom smiles. "Just be faithful even if she's not your girlfriend. Don't go to those parties and don't have pictures of yourself with girls posted all over the internet. Trust me, she'll be looking for them even if she says she's not into you. Once she sees that you're not dating anyone else, she might change her mind."

"And what if she doesn't?" I ask.

Mom shrugs. "Then it wasn't meant to be."

"I don't like that answer very much."

She laughs. "Well, that's just life, son. Sometimes you get the girl and sometimes you don't."

I inhale and let it out in a huff. I know she's right but I don't have to like it. I want Bree in my life. I want her to be mine. I also want to be successful in my career. Why can't I have both?

My phone rings. I pull it out of my pocket and see the face of my manager on the call screen. Dammit. I answer the call while my mom watches me curiously.

Marcus is in a great mood as he tells me that I've been offered a commercial deal for an energy drink that partners with Team Loco. They need me in the studio in LA tomorrow morning. It pays thirty thousand dollars for about four hours of work. Holy shit.

I can't turn that down, but it does mean flying back tonight and missing out on my chance of seeing Bree these next two days. Marcus doesn't really give me a choice to accept the commercial or not. He just tells me the energy drink company has paid for my flight to Cali in the morning and that there will be a car at the airport to pick me up. I get off the phone and tell Mom the good news.

"Wow!" she gushes. "Thirty grand? That's not bad."

I nod. "It's not bad at all, and yet here I am feeling like taking this job means I'll never get Bree back."

Mom frowns and pats my leg. "You just need to do the best you can, son. Your career is important, and if you and Bree are meant to be an item then she'll understand that."

I try to visualize my life if things were different. If Bree and I had started dating years ago and then I got famous, would she be okay with it? Probably. I don't think it's my career that's keeping us apart. I think it's my past. My history of being a womanizer who never settles down.

"I think you're right, Mom," I say. "I'm going to prove to Bree that I can be loyal even if she's not my girl yet. And then maybe one day she will be."

CHAPTER 22

Bree

Dad wakes up after a week in the hospital. It's tough on me to see him like this. He's confused and in pain. While Mama and I try our best to comfort him, I can tell it doesn't really help. Mama pulled me aside the day before he woke up and we made a promise to be very positive and upbeat around Dad for the time being. We're not going to mention how he almost died, and we won't mention his long recovery process. No matter what, we're not going to talk about money or our fears or anything. We're going to be a supportive front so my dad can get better.

A couple nights ago, I'd gone home for another shower and I dug through all of the household bills. I added up what the important stuff costs on a normal month and was happy to find that Mama and I make just enough money to cover the bills. I'll need to pick up as many shifts at the motocross track as Mrs. Sam will let me, and I'll also find a job. Right now I just need any job. Even flipping burgers at Skeeter's would be better than nothing right now. I'll save my dream job search for after Dad gets better.

In the meantime though, things are tight. Mama canceled all of her cleaning jobs this week to be with Dad. Luckily her clients are all being very supportive. A few of them paid her even though she couldn't clean their house and said to consider it a bonus for years of her hard work.

People in this town can be really nice. I'm glad I decided to stay here. Now I just hope I'll never run into the guy who broke my heart again. I might not be able to handle that much longer. Hopefully I'll move on. Maybe I'll meet another guy someday.

It's Monday morning and I'm standing in line in the hospital cafeteria getting some pancakes for my mom and me. The eggs here are gross and the bacon is soggy so the pancakes are your best bet. I bring the food back upstairs to the ICU and Mama and I eat it in the waiting room. I sit on the opposite side of the room from where I saw Zach sleeping that day. My eyes keep drifting over to that chair. I can't believe he did something like that. What did he think my reaction would be?

Was I supposed to hug him and say all is forgiven? I can't have a relationship with a guy who is just going to leave. I can't have a relationship with a guy who doesn't even know how to be a boyfriend. All Zach knows is how to hook up and then call a girl a cab.

I grimace and shove a bite of pancakes in my mouth.

"It's your turn to go home," Mama says after we've eaten.

"Already?" I say. We've been alternating days on who goes home to shower and take a nap in our own bed, that way one of us is always here with Dad. I feel bad leaving him, but getting some sleep in my own bed is so much better than sleeping hunched over in the pleather chair in Dad's hospital room.

"I went home yesterday," Mama says.

I nod, and then a yawn escapes me. My body definitely wants that nap. "Okay," I say. "I think I'll stop by the track and ask Mrs. Sam if I can work more shifts."

Mama nods. "That's a good idea."

It's been a week and Dad is going to be okay, so I know it's time to start working more and sitting in the hospital less. Any money I can bring in will be good for us.

I say goodbye to my dad, who is half asleep from the drugs they have him on, and then I hug Mama and head outside to where the rest of the world is still carrying on like usual outside of this hospital. I get in my car and drive home, mentally adding up how much money I can make if I work every race day and a few practice days during the week.

I almost don't even notice the truck in my driveway, and when I do, it's too late. I can't keep driving and pretend I didn't see him.

My knees shake as I park my car and step out. Zach is sitting on my front porch, a massive bouquet of pink roses in his lap.

What the hell is he doing here? It's been a week. I was finally starting to feel slightly less heartbroken.

I grip my keys in my hands and take a deep breath to steady myself.

Zach stands up, his eyes never leaving mine as I walk the short distance from the driveway to the porch.

"I thought I kicked you out," I say.

He holds out the flowers toward me. "I don't give up after one lost race."

I take the flowers and glance down at their beautiful petals. Then I meet his gaze. "Life isn't like motocross races," I say.

"Trust me," Zach says as his eyes sweep over me. "I know. Life is so much better than racing. At least, it is when I'm with you."

The flowers are heavy. There must be three dozen roses in this bouquet. I shove my key in the front door and unlock it, then venture inside to set the flowers on the counter. Zach stands on the porch watching me.

"You know you're crazy right?" I say, trying to keep my heart from pounding. "You've only known me like a month."

"Can I come inside?" he asks.

I shrug. "Sure."

He steps inside and closes the door behind him. Immediately the bright sunlight fades away and my cozy living room feels ten times smaller now that it's just the two of us standing here.

"We might have only known each other a month," he says, slowly closing the distance between us. "But we've been in the same world our whole lives. We both grew up at this track. You know motocross as well as I do. You're a part of the community, just like me." He takes one final step toward me and now we're just inches apart. He reaches up and cups my cheek in his hand. I don't know why, but I let him.

Those gorgeous blue eyes peer into mine. "Let's buy the track from old man Perkins."

My eyes widen. "What?"

He smiles. "Maybe not today. But someday. Let's buy it and run it ourselves. You can put your business skills to work and we can fix up the place, turn it into a nationally known race track. We can do it all together. Here, at home. In the motocross community."

"You're insane," I say, but I'd be lying if I said the idea doesn't sound awesome. "Buying the place will probably cost a fortune."

"We can afford it," he says. At some point, his other hand grabbed my waist. Now we're just inches apart and my heart is racing and I can't find a single part of me that wants him to go away.

"We?" I say, recalling his words. "*You* might be able to afford to buy sixty acres and a business, but *I* can't."

He places a soft kiss on my forehead. "We can afford it if we're together," he whispers. "I just need a few more years of professional racing and then we'll have the money."

"You keep saying *we*," I say. "We're not a *we*."

His eyes stare into mine. "We could be."

I swallow. "I'm just supposed to blink and forgive everything? And just be okay with everything?"

He shakes his head. "No, I don't expect that. Which is why I'm going to prove it to you. As long as it takes, Bree. I'll prove that I can be faithful. I only want you. No one else."

My defenses are cracking. I can feel it. All these walls are tumbling down. "So what now?" I say, trying to sound bold even though I'm crumbling.

"You don't have to say anything. You don't have to agree or promise to be my girl or anything," he whispers, his lips just inches from mine. "Just let me prove it to you. I'll do whatever it takes to make you my girl. However long it takes. I'll do it."

I bite my bottom lip. "What if it takes a long time to gain my trust?"

He shrugs. "Then it takes a long time."

Something deep in my gut tells me to believe him. I don't know why, and maybe I'm stupid, but I don't think I am. I can feel it. He just feels right. Like Zach Pena was made to be my soul mate. My everything.

That doesn't mean I won't make him work for it.

"Fine," I say, taking a small step backward to give myself room to breathe. "Let's do this."

His gorgeous lips break into a grin. "Really?"

I nod, unable to hide my own grin. "If you keep your promises and you don't let me down then… yeah, I'll be your girlfriend."

He puts his hands together in a praying motion and tips his head back in a quick thank you to the heavens. "Oh, Bree," he says, smiling so big it makes me laugh. "You won't regret this."

I slide my hands up his chest and hook them around his neck. "I better not."

His strong hands are on my waist, holding me close to him. "Can I kiss you?" he breathes, his lips just inches from mine. A fire roars in my belly, and I want so much more than a kiss from this man.

"Mhm," I say. "But not here."

"Then where?" he whispers.

I give him a devilish grin. "My bedroom."

His eyes narrow mischievously and then he scoops me up, carrying me straight to my bedroom. He kicks the door closed behind us and then drops me on my bed.

"Take off your clothes," I say, reaching for my own shirt.

He grins, and pulls his shirt over his head in one quick movement. "Yes, ma'am."

CHAPTER 24

ZACH

2 months later

I run my hand down the seat of my dirt bike. Team Loco recently changed all the graphics to this slick royal blue and silver color scheme. It looks great. My gear is all new as well, and this is the first time I'm wearing it. I tug on my jersey and tuck it into my pants, liking the new silver color. It's a weird time for the team to change their look. Usually they change up the colors at the start of the year.

Today is the last race of the summer season. In two weeks, the fall circuit begins and I've already scored my spot on the team. The fall circuit is more prestigious than the summer series since we'll race at bigger tracks to larger audiences. All of the uber-famous motocross racers will be there, whereas some of them take off during the summer. But today's race is the most important one of the summer season. Jett and I are tied for first place. Whoever wins the race today will be the winner of the whole summer series.

Luckily, that means a win for Team Loco no matter what. But my girl will be here tonight and I'm hoping to win for her. The idea of her flying all the way out to Vegas to watch me lose doesn't work for me. I need to win.

I walk over to where my teammates are hanging out under the Team Loco canopy next to our bikes. We're in the large parking lot area of the arena and the fans haven't been allowed inside yet, so it's only VIPs in here now.

Aiden is back, but his arm is still in a cast and he's not cleared to ride for a few more weeks. He says he's here for moral support, but I think he's sick of seeing his family back at home. Like me, he feels more comfortable being in the world of motocross. He lounges in a chair wearing dark sunglasses, his casted arm resting on his stomach.

Jett and Clay are huddled around Clay's phone, watching a YouTube video. I don't know what they're watching, but I can hear dirt bike sounds coming from the small phone speaker so I guess it's a video of themselves.

"Oh my God," Keanna says. I turn around to see her and Bree walking back to our canopy. Keanna puts one hand to her heart while the other one holds a pink cup with a thick blue straw. "These smoothies are amazing!"

"I know, right?" Clay says. "They're like crack. But healthy crack."

"What flavor did you get?" Jett asks Keanna. She holds out her cup and he takes a sip.

I turn my attention to Bree. "Having fun?" I ask, pressing a quick kiss to her lips.

"Mhm," she says, sipping from her smoothie. "I don't know what I'd do if Keanna weren't here to show me around."

"I'm glad you two are getting along."

She smiles up at me. Things have been so good between us. We've had to be long distance for several weeks, but I've been flying home after every race just to hang out with her until I have to fly back each weekend. This is the first time she's come with me to watch me race. Her dad is finally home from the hospital and he's doing much better. He has a couple of months until he starts physical therapy, but we're all rooting for him to be okay.

The Perkins started an online fundraiser for him and the donations have been coming in nonstop. Jett, Clay, and Aiden were nice enough to post about it on their social media pages and now their fans are donating too. I know it won't lessen the pain of recovery, but now Bree's family won't have to stress over how they'll pay the bills. And because of it, Bree finally felt okay taking a few days off work to travel with me.

I pull her in close and kiss her lips, which now taste like strawberries and kiwi. "I'm so glad you're here," I say just low enough for only us to hear.

"Me too," she says with a grin that makes her so cute I could die.

I haven't told her the good news yet because we haven't had much time alone since we flew out here yesterday morning. But two days ago, I called Grant Perkins and talked to him about what his plans were for when he retires. He said he'd never thought about it, but if he's going to sell the track to anyone, he'd pick me. We talked about how there's still plenty of time until the day comes, but he knows that I want to buy the track. I want to finish out my professional racing career and then settle down in my hometown with the girl of my dreams. We can build our future at Hopewell Motocross Park. It's going to be amazing. I can't wait to tell her.

Marcus rides up on his golf cart and brings several boxes of catered food for lunch. The races don't start for a few more hours, so it's the perfect time to eat. In an hour, the fans will be let into the pit area and I'll be sighing autographs. The nervous tingle I always get just before a race starts to settle in. It doesn't matter how many times I've raced, I still get a little nervous before it. Not that I'll ever admit that to anyone.

We eat lunch and then Keanna and Bree decide to get another smoothie from the smoothie food truck. As they walk off, Marcus nudges me in the elbow. "You did good with that one," he says, nodding toward Bree. "I like her. She's keeping you grounded and it shows in the way you race. You're more focused."

"Thanks," I say. "I'm lucky to have her."

"That's for damn sure," Marcus snorts. "A girl like that is too good for you."

I roll my eyes and he punches me playfully in the arm, then he heads back into the large motorhome behind us. Marcus prefers to stay in the air conditioning as long as possible.

When the pits are opened to the public, all of Team Loco lines up and sits behind tables that separate us from the fans. We all have a stack of posters of ourselves that we sign for everyone. I'm sitting between Clay and Jett. Jett is usually the most popular of the whole team, probably because of his dad's fame. But today I'm getting just as many squealing fans and people who want to lean across the table to take a photo with me. It feels so good to know I haven't totally ruined my career.

I glance back at Bree between signing posters. She's sitting next to Keanna and she gives me a little wave. I hope I'll win this race and make her proud. But even if I don't, I know she'll still be there for me, still cheering me on and supporting me. I wave back at my girlfriend and then turn back around and smile at the little boy who is eagerly waiting for my autograph. For the first time in my life, I feel like things are finally going the way I want them to.

I've never been happier.

Thank you for reading Taming Zach! If you enjoyed the book, please consider leaving a review on the site where you bought this book. It doesn't even have to be long; just one sentence helps out a lot!

Don't miss the next book in the Team Loco Series

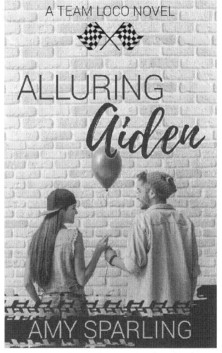

*

Want to get an email when Amy's next book is released? Sign up for her newsletter here and get exclusive access to giveaways, new releases, and more!
Sign up here: http://eepurl.com/bTmkPX

About the Author

Amy Sparling is the author of The Summer Unplugged Series, Ella's Twisted Senior Year, Deadbeat & other awesome books for teens and the teenagers at heart. She loves coffee, the beach, and swooning over book boyfriends.
Amy loves getting messages from her readers and responds to every single one! Connect with her on one of the links below.

Connect with Amy online!

Website: AmySparling.com
Twitter: @Amy_Sparling
Instagram: @writeamysparling
Goodreads: goodreads.com/Amy_Sparling
Wattpad: AmySparlingWrites

36359191R00162

Made in the USA
Columbia, SC
24 November 2018